Spooky Girl

Allan Evans

This book is dedicated to my daughter,
the real-life Abbey—and to all the ghosts
that have haunted our home.

Life has never been boring with all of you around.

1 | HAUNTED HAPPENINGS

I hate dead people.

Shivering as the hairs stand on the back of my neck, I know what I need to do. The basement stairwell is pitch dark and of course nothing happens when I flip the light switch. Nothing in my life goes that easy. The house is silent except for the sound of my own breathing. Still, I am not alone.

Trying to be ninja, I slip carefully down the wooden stairs. The third step lets out a slow creak as I ease my full weight onto it. The fourth step doesn't do me any favors either, not that it makes a difference. Someone—or something—is waiting for me.

A solitary figure stands at the base of the stairs. An old woman dressed in a flowing vintage gown beckons me to proceed. A gust of wind kicks up—kind of strange considering I'm inside a basement—and my hair swirls around my face. The woman stands in front of me, her skin the color of a pale brown paper bag with faint shades of olive green, any trace of pink long forgotten. Though her face is shrouded in shadows, I make out the outlines of the ancient furnace hulking behind the old woman. The transparency of her drab, colorless clothing makes it evident she's only partially here in our world.

Yeah, I see dead people.

"Why are you here?" I ask, waiting. I get nothing in return. Experience has taught me not to expect much—if anything—in the way of verbal interaction in these situations. Communication being a two-way street, I want this thing to know I'm aware of its presence and I'm not happy about it.

If this woman wants me down in the basement, she must have a reason. Let's have it then. I ask my question again, "Why are you here?" Stepping right up to the woman, the cold is so intense, I can't help but shiver. As close as I am, I can't see her eyes. A veil of shadow covers her face and I'm left staring into a pit of darkness. Her hand slowly comes up and reaches for my cheek. It takes everything I have to hold my ground.

A sensation of vertigo hits me as the woman's long-dead hand makes contact with my skin. Images of angry faces and a violent struggle race through my head, a chaotic whirl speeding by too fast to comprehend. I need this to stop before I get swept away, unable to process my own thoughts. It takes every ounce of willpower to raise my hand. Drawing strength from my momentum, I focus everything on the spirit's hand and wrap my fingers around the pale wrist. I'm actually able to make contact with the icy cold skin, ripping the hand from my cheek.

The image freight train careening through my head comes to a screeching halt and I start breathing again. This dead woman wants me to know about her death, but there's nothing I can do. Clearly she died ages ago.

Without warning, her hand comes at me, shifting focus from my cheek to my throat. Possessing a strength I couldn't have foreseen, she brings me to my knees as I fight to keep the hand at a safe distance. It's my own fault as I'm the one who enabled this contact. Lesson learned. Twisting violently, I let her hand shoot past me toward the concrete floor and slide my hand from her grip. Contact lost, her power over me diminishes immediately. Though not for a second do I believe the threat is over. I need to end this.

"Time for you to leave. You're not wanted here. Now go!" I shout. The breeze has now become a whirlwind and the overhead light blinks on, burning supernaturally bright. With a loud pop, the bulb shatters leaving me covered in shards of glass and plunges me once again into darkness. The old woman gone.

I really hate dead people.

Opening the door at the top of the stairs, I step into the light. Squinting to see, I make out a tall figure across the room, facing away from me. My eyes adjusting to the light, I recognize my father standing at our kitchen sink, his hands deep in the soapy water as he cleans up our dinner dishes. "Hey, Abbey," he calls over his shoulder. "What's going on in the basement?"

"Nothing," I answer. "I thought I heard something down there."

"I hope those squirrels haven't found their way back into the basement. That's the trouble with these old houses."

Fighting back a smile, I reassure him. "No, I didn't see a single squirrel. Quiet as a graveyard down there." I don't like lying to my father, however some things are best left unsaid. My father doesn't need to know his daughter is a certifiable spook magnet and that my childhood ghostly experiences have continued—let alone become so prevalent.

My name is Abbey, and like most 14-year-old girls you meet, I'm relatively normal—at least until you get to know me. And then all bets are off.

As you have likely picked up on by now, ghosts like me. Okay, "like" might be putting too much of a positive spin on it. They absolutely are drawn to me—like a fat kid is drawn to a plate of donuts.

There's a picture taken on my first birthday, I've got chocolate frosting smeared all over my smiling face and my great-grandmother looms behind me in the background. My recently deceased great-grandmother. Guess she really didn't want to miss my party.

My mom told me a story about when I was young. She said I had been sitting on the floor playing with my dolls and the door behind me had closed by itself. My mom had put down her book and opened the door. As soon as she was back on the couch, the door closed again. Frustrated, she got back up and placed a large book against the door to prop it open. The moment she was back sitting on the couch with her book, the door slammed shut again. Mom was shocked to find the door locked and the book returned to its place on the bookshelf. This is how my life has always been—things have never been normal around me.

As I grew older, my mother would get upset when I would tell her about these visits. She really seemed troubled and worried about me. Sometimes she would cry and I didn't like that at all. After awhile when I was old enough to start figuring things out, I decided it was better not to tell her every time a ghost made an appearance. I stopped telling my father most of the time, too. I think maybe he still knew, but at least he had his plausible deniability.

There's an art to keeping a straight face when a ghost walks into the room and you don't want the others around you to know. It takes supreme focus to keep talking to your mother about her day when a ghost passes through a closed door, glances your way and then does a double take. I had one walk right up to me and was waving his hand right in front of my face the way—the way someone would check if a person really could see through their super dark sunglasses.

These days, I try to shelter my father as best as I can. Since it's just the two of us now, he already has a lot on his plate. I'll always be his little girl and he'll always be the person I look up to most. Which is exactly why my father's announcement came as such a blow.

"No way. I have to spend the rest of my summer vacation in River Falls? Wisconsin would be my last choice of places to finish out the summer. Why can't I come with you?"

My father gazed at me with tender eyes. I could tell it wasn't easy on him either to leave me behind. "I really can't bring you this time. I'm going to be on a military base and there's not a place for children there. I did check, I really did."

My father is an investigative journalist who travels the world writing books and magazine stories chronicling the mysteries of our time. Whether it was psychic healers, UFOs, the Loch Ness Monster, Bigfoot, a government cover-up of an invisibility experiment gone horribly wrong, or off to Easter Island to examine the large stone heads, my father has been on some amazing journeys. "Look, it's just six short weeks and then I'll be home and you'll start high school."

Arms folded, I hold my ground. "That's the problem. You can't send me off to church camp the summer before school. High school is important. I need to prepare."

A pained expression briefly colors his face. "I hate to disappoint you."

"Well, yeah. Adults have disappointed me all my life. Remember how much I liked Santa until I found out about all the amazing crap he gave my rich friends for Christmas?" I can't help but giggle.

My father gives me a chuckle. "I also remember that you got over it. And besides, it's not like it's really a camp," he says. "There are no leaky tents or run-down cabins. You'll be staying at River Falls College, living in the dorms. Camp Agape is the Cadillac of church camps."

"Camp Agape? Camps should have cool names like Camp Runamuck. Kathleen went to a camp last summer by a dried up lake named Camp Lakebegone. That was a cool name."

"Okay, but a few short weeks at church camp will be good for you," he says, giving me a look, "you may learn a thing or two." I narrow my eyes at him, but he plows on. "And besides, your mother would have wanted this for you."

Eyes down, I can't look at him. He's not playing fair. "I hate it when you play that card."

My father smiles a warm smile, not at all gloating—lucky for him. "I'm sure you'll have a summer vacation to remember for the rest of your life."

"That's exactly what I'm worried about," I call over my shoulder as I retreat to my room.

And as it turned out, I was right to be worried.

2 | WHERE IS THE LOVE?

River Falls College is roughly 30 miles from the Twin Cities and is located along the beautiful Kinnickinnic River. The Kinnie is well known in the area for its trout fishing. The town of River Falls has approximately 13,000 residents according to the last census and nearly 15 percent of that population was found to be living below the poverty line. According to pretty much anyone who has visited from the Twin Cities, River Falls is officially a small town.

One thing people learn about me is that I do my homework. I don't like going into situations unprepared. If I'm going to be stuck here for the next several months, I'm at least going to be smart about it. I read as much as I could find about River Falls last night.

"You'll be alright checking in?" my father asks as we get out of the car. "Sorry to just drop you off on the curb, but I'm in danger of missing my flight." The torrential downpour we encountered driving through the St. Croix valley had put him behind his less-than-organized schedule. I had been totally surprised when we were able to leave the house only twenty minutes behind schedule this morning. Typically, every departure is delayed because my father would have to run back in the house for "just one more thing." With a glance at the gray sky, he says, "At least the rain has stopped, we managed to get ahead of it."

Three minutes later, after apologizing profusely for not escorting me inside, I'm left alone with a stack of luggage watching my father's tail lights round the corner and disappear for the next six weeks. Heavy sigh. Always a master of timing, the rain chooses this moment to catch up and the downpour hits. Sometimes life is not at all fair. "Thanks a lot," I say out loud to no one in particular as I gather my things to look for shelter.

I try walking backward dragging the pair of suitcases by the handles and the duffels by the straps. However this is clearly not working, evidenced by my right foot now entangled in the bike rack. Okay, time to regroup. Crisscrossing the duffel bags over each shoulder frees my hands to carry the suitcases. But which way? With the rain coming down as hard as it is, the buildings are indistinct shapes, none of them looking particularly inviting. Almost on cue, a bell begins to chime in the clock overlooking a nearby building. Any port in the storm, my father would say, and so I turn that way, anxious to get out of the rain. Walking up the sidewalk, I pause to look at the clock, which is continuing its loud chiming. Why would the clock be chiming now, when the time is 10:37? This could be an odd place to spend my summer, I think as I push through the massive wooden door.

Unsure which direction to go, I stand there feeling the rain pouring off me. "Starting to look like rain out there," a girl's voice says behind me, a hint of a French accent in her voice. I jump, startled by the proximity of the girl. I hadn't heard anyone approaching.

"Yeah, I'll have to find my umbrella," I reply, looking down at the small lake spreading out beneath me. Shivering, all I can do is laugh. "I'm the new girl, Abbey."

With a dramatic flair, she holds out her hand. "Truly. As in truly madly deeply." Truly is a thin girl, several inches below me in height, with pinned-up blonde hair and glasses. She is wearing an oversize powder blue sweater—though from the look of her, unless she bought her clothes from the children's department, almost everything would be oversized. "So sorry I have to run, but you'll find Mr. Johnson through those doors over there," she says, gesturing across the lobby.

"Thanks," I say turning back, but Truly is gone.

The group of teenagers is large, maybe twenty or so sitting on the floor, all staring at me. Some of them have their mouths open. Haven't they ever seen someone so wet, they're moments away from pneumonia? A grownup has his back to me as he loudly addresses the group. He pauses, realizing there has been a change in the room. It's been my experience adults don't like losing control of things, and so it's no surprise when he turns around and fixes me with the sort of expression you might make when you first notice a particularly bad odor has entered the room. The man is older, and has spiky brown hair with a bad dye job, as if he is trying to look younger than his AARP card might indicate. I smile at him, trying to look both sweet and vulnerable. He doesn't appear to notice this, as his attention is instead focused on the puddle spreading beneath me onto the gym floor. Looking up at me, there is a cold fury clouding his face. This is not a man who radiates joy.

"And you are?" he asks as his greeting. "Wet. And late. Sorry about the puddle," I say, looking down. "It's looking like rain."

There is a snicker from somewhere in the group. The adult in front of me is not amused, however. "Your name, please." At least I get the courtesy of a please.

"Abbey," I reply simply.

"Ahh, Miss Hill. Camp started yesterday, as you know."

"But I just found out yesterday I was coming here today." Great, I'm here for five minutes and I already feel like I'm behind.

"Nevertheless, you are still late. You'll have to wait to get settled in after we are through here. Why don't you have a seat." Not a question, he gestures to the side of the group. I drop my bags where I stand and find a spot to sit by the edge of the group. The boy next to me gives me a wary look and slides away, putting some extra space between us.

"Camp Agape," I mutter to myself, shaking my head, "where is the love?"

The boy next to me starts to cough, though I suspect he's trying to cover his laugh. Mr. Johnson shoots the boy a look and then clearing his throat, speaks. "Physical training is vitally important, as you'll need both a strong mind and a strong body to resist the temptations that come your way. Having the confidence to meet these challenges head on will carry you through the battles to come. You are here," he says, looking around the room, "because you've lost these battles in the past. I'm here to tell you just because it's happened before doesn't mean it has to happen again. Work hard for the next two months and life will be different for you. You will be a new person, with a new attitude. You will have the strength to fight back from now on. Okay, Kirsten, you're first. Go climb the rope. And don't stop until you reach the top."

A skinny girl gets to her feet, nervously looking around the room and approaches the rope. She pauses at the bottom, gazing up the knotted rope to the ceiling twenty feet above. She looks less than confident as she ever-so-slowly reaches for the thick rope with her small hands.

"It won't bite, Kirsten. Climb," he barks. She jumps at the sound of his voice and is halfway up the rope in a matter of moments. "Okay," he says looking at us with a gleefully evil stare, "get into groups by the ropes. Everyone will need to climb the rope five times each." Groans echo around the gymnasium. So far, this is not the church camp experience I had been expecting. Maybe we'll be singing Kumbaya around the campfire a little later, but I'm starting to have my doubts. It wouldn't surprise me to hear this is the only camp on the planet without a campfire. This is definitely an odd place.

3 | THE SISTERS' GRIMM

My shoulders are sore, my thighs burn and my hands feel like I stuck them into a running garbage disposal. Forcing me to lug my suitcases in this condition could constitute cruel and unusual punishment in some of the more enlightened countries around the world. However, here in River Falls, you have to carry your burdens alone. Moving slowly, I bring up the rear of the pack. The group as a whole looks tired and no one says a word as we make our way across the campus. The rain has stopped, but the wetness lives on, as I trudge through puddles unable to lift my feet high enough to avoid soaking them.

We leave the road and turn up a sidewalk heading toward a four-story building. The older brick building looks neglected, giving me the mental picture of moldy mattresses and leaky faucets that drip endlessly. Of course there will be dusty pictures of long dead professors adorning the peeling wallpaper walls. I can survive all this, I tell myself. I can do all things …

I stop dead in my tracks. "I can't do this," I say out loud, dropping my suitcases.

The sign in front of the building reads, "Grimm Hall." This is a sign if there ever was one. No way am I going to live in a building named Grimm Hall. Foreboding and bleak, this is not where I want to lay my head each night for the next two months.

"C'mon, I'll give you a hand with these," a welcoming voice offers. I find Kirsten, the rope queen, next to me. "It's not as bad inside as it looks from out here. I've only counted four rats so far."

My head whips around, and no doubt my jaw is open so wide that a bear might consider my mouth a suitable location for hibernation. The twinkle in her eye clues me in I've been a victim of her charming sense of humor. I close my mouth. "Funny," I say without a trace of a smile. "You should get a job as a standup comedian. It would be fun watching you starve."

"Believe me, this isn't how I want to spend my summer vacation, either," Kirsten says, totally ignoring my comment. "I understand why you don't want to be here, I'm not much of a small town kind of girl, either. There's surprisingly little nightlife in River Falls. But you're stuck here just like the rest of us and we'll have to make the best of it." Kirsten starts up the sidewalk, carrying my suitcases with little difficulty. I assume Kirsten's expecting me to follow her, as she never turns around, climbing the steps two at a time.

Fine. I'll follow the perky rope queen. But I hate it here. I don't want to spend a single night here in the Grimm dungeon, living with the rats— real or imaginary. I get the shivers, as I can't help but picture being woken up by the touch of something crawling along my legs under the covers, something so terrifying, that I'm frozen in place as the damp and scratchy thing tickles my bare legs as it creeps further up. I shudder, trying vainly to push the image out of my head and reluctantly hurry to catch up to my suitcases.

"You don't want to take the elevator," Kirsten warns when I catch up.

"You have to wait forever and they make noises that, well, put it this way, don't inspire confidence. I prefer to be confident that when I step into an elevator, I'll be able to walk back out of it." The stairs have a musty smell but otherwise aren't too bad. My aversion to the stair climbers at the gym come back to haunt me once again, as I have to pause for oxygen on the second floor landing. We continue all the way up to the fourth floor.

Giant sheets of draped plastic block off the construction area. "They're remodeling this middle section, so watch your step," Kirsten says as she pushes through the plastic. The hallway carpet has been pulled up; the room doors have been removed and are leaning against the walls as we make our way down the narrow hall. Generally, there looks to be a lot of work still to be completed. "I've heard there are a number of buildings under construction on campus. This isn't as bad as some of the others."

We come to another wall of plastic, and I am thankful we are going to be living in the remodeled section. As I hold the sheet open for Kirsten and my suitcases, I realize my mistake. This is the old section, and they have yet to start work here. I had the peeling wallpaper part correct, but there aren't any photographs of long deceased professors on the wall. The walls are bare, with the occasional whiter rectangle spaced every few feet apart. Ahh, the pictures had been there but have been removed in anticipation of the upcoming remodel. The doors have little signs cut in the shape of a tent taped to them, two on each door. Written in Sharpie markers are the resident's names, all girls.

At the end of the hall, we come to a door, and I find my name written on one of the construction paper tents. The name on the other says Stacia, apparently my roommate for the summer. I hope she is normal, but I wouldn't put any money on it. There hasn't been a normal minute since I got here. Hoping for the best, I open the door to find a small room with beds on opposite sides and a girl lying on her stomach on the far one. Stacia doesn't appear to notice us, as I can hear the music from her ear buds all the way over here. Kirsten drops the suitcases on the floor by my bed and says she'll catch up with me at lunch, leaving me alone with my new roommate.

I'm torn, as Stacia doesn't see me standing here. Should I try to catch her attention or just wait until I'm noticed? I decide to unpack and wait until she sees me. It doesn't take long to throw my jeans and t-shirts into the dresser drawers, and she still hasn't looked my way. I've always been impatient—so anyone who knows me wouldn't be surprised when a rolled up pair of socks slips out of my hand and accidentally flies across the room, hitting Stacia. She jumps, clearly startled. In my defense, I absolutely hate being ignored. She pulls the buds from her ears, turning toward me—and I'm stunned. It's Truly.

"Truly, what are you doing here? I thought my roommate was Stacia—at least that's what the sign on our door reads."

Sitting up, she says, "I get that a lot. Truly is my twin sister. We don't always get along, so we're in different rooms."

The French accent is absent, but otherwise the two sisters are identical. "How come she has an accent and you don't?"

Smiling, Stacia nods. "I get that question a lot, as well. Truly lives with our father in Paris, while I live with our mother in Lake Elmo. She claims to be the smarter of the two of us, but I like to think I'm the better looking one."

That's a mighty thin hope to hang your hat on when you're an identical twin. But I'm not going to be the one to burst her bubble. "Sorry about the socks, I can be a little clumsy sometimes." I shrug.

Sitting up, she says, "I could see how that might happen. But I'm guessing you're not telling me the truth either." Stacia is a slight girl, shorter than me. Most girls her size would fear a strong a gust of wind, but Stacia exhibits an intensity that quite possibly would make the wind think twice about bothering her.

Her eyes burn holes in me as she waits for my response.

I'm not sure how to answer Stacia, as she is difficult to read. I can't tell if she's serious or not. She looks grumpy with a side of psycho thrown in for good measure. I decide the truth is my best option. "I may have tossed the socks to get your attention." I pause for effect. "I can be a badass that way."

Stacia nods. "Don't even tell me how badass you are until you know how many Nutella packets I stole at hotel breakfasts in Florida over spring break." She holds my gaze.

I'm not sure I've seen anyone blur the line between "not a morning person" and serial killer quite like my new roommate. But I nod and say, "Yeah, I can totally see that." This appears to make her happy, as Stacia gives me a great big grin.

"We'll have a great time hanging out this summer. Want to go explore?" she asks, changing topics abruptly. Stacia's smile promises more than a quiet walk around campus.

"How can I resist?" I ask as we head for the door, jumping at the opportunity to check out my new world.

4 | TOUGH LOVING

Crabtree Hall looms at the end of residence hall row. Out wandering, we had walked past Parker Hall and saw McMillan Hall in the opposite direction. The entire Crabtree Hall building is closed for construction which makes it interesting and worthy of exploring. Blatantly ignoring the Off Limits, Closed for Construction and Do Not Enter signs, we enter the building through the front door. The smell of sawdust hits me right away, the scent immediately triggering memories of my grandfather working in his shop. He had built a woodworking shop in his garage and would spend hours building benches, shelves and various home improvement projects. Whenever we visited, I would say a quick hi to grandma and then head for the garage to assist him in his woodworking. I may not have been much help, but he was patient and funny, and we always had a wonderful time together. I loved my grandpa. Those were some of my favorite memories of all time.

"Planet Earth to Abbey. Anybody home?" Stacia asks, waving a hand in front of my face.

"Sorry, I stopped to think and forgot to start again. The sawdust smell reminded me of my grandfather," I explain.

"Really? Sawdust?" Stacia asks. "He certainly had unusual tastes in colognes." She grins at me.

"Funny girl." Turning the corner, we head down a hallway with no particular destination, just the desire to explore.

Strident voices ahead break up the stillness. As we move down the hall, it becomes evident there is an argument in progress. We stop outside an open door, staying close to the wall, not wanting to be discovered eavesdropping.

"I'm not going back up there. I'll work down here or over in Grimm, but that's all." The voice has an accent, Hispanic possibly.

"It's not up to you. As your site supervisor, you go where I need you to go. Simple." This voice is older sounding than the first one. It also has an annoyingly superior quality about it.

There's a moment of hesitation, and then the first voice replies. "I…I can't."

"Are you afraid?" A mocking tone.

I look at Stacia and her eyebrow goes up. I'm intrigued. Why would he be afraid?

"Things move by themselves. I'm on the floor, working on the trim and set down my hammer. It's right beside me. I reach for it again, and it's no longer there."

"So you forgot where you set your hammer." The site supervisor is not exactly sympathetic.

"You don't get it," his voice is sounding more agitated. "I'm still on my knees after using my hammer and now my hammer is across the room—on the counter. There's no way my hammer moved by itself from the floor to the counter. I swear I was the only person in the room."

Stacia's mouth is hanging open.

The first voice continues. "I can't keep working here. Something's not right up there." The voice is getting louder; he's headed for the door. Crap, he's headed for us. Stacia and I look at each other, panicked.

The second voice saves us. "Hold on, Juan. I'll have you start on the east wing." We don't wait to hear what he says next, as we are dashing down the hall anxious to get away from the two men. Outside, we finally pause to catch our breath.

"That was close," Stacia says. "They almost found us."

I look at Stacia. "Didn't you think his story was a bit strange? Hammers don't move by themselves."

"My mother always said superstition is the invention of an uneducated mind. The construction guy probably forgot he'd left his hammer on the counter." We start walking back towards Grimm Hall, our exploration over for the time being.

I'm shaking my head. "I don't know. I've seen some strange things, and this feels like one of those moments. I have to say, this is the oddest church camp I've ever visited."

It takes a moment before I notice Stacia is no longer walking alongside me. I glance back to find her stopped in her tracks. "Did you say church camp?" she asks with an odd look on her face.

"Yeah, my father said Camp Agape would be good for me. It's not how I wanted to spend my summer, though."

"Oh my," Stacia blurts and then begins to laugh. You know how when someone keeps laughing and you can't help but join in? This wasn't one of those times.

"What?" I demand. "What is it?" Though at this point, I'm not so sure I want to know the answer.

Stacia catches her breath, wiping away a tear from the corner of her eye and officially ruins my summer. "Camp Agape ended last week. This is Camp ToughLove."

"Camp ToughLove?"

Nodding, Stacia continues, her voice slow and measured, as though reading from a brochure. "Welcome to Camp ToughLove, the boot camp where troubled teens come to strengthen their minds, bodies and spirits in a highly disciplined arena." She rests a hand on my shoulder, which I take to be a gesture of sympathy. "And the emphasis here is squarely on discipline. This will not be a pleasant summer vacation at church camp."

5 | BUNKIN' WITH A HORSE RUSTLER?

I am absolutely numb: a Bachelor candidate, totally mind-dead sort of numb. Lying on my bed staring at the ceiling, I try to make sense of my predicament. How could this have happened? My father would not have knowingly sent me to a boot camp, would he? It's not like I've really been a troubled teen. Sure, I don't like to clean my room, and my father always has to remind me to put away my dinner dishes, and I do watch some cable shows I'm not supposed to watch. And—oh my God, I am a troubled teen!

My mind races as I steal a glance toward Stacia. I wonder what she's in for? Am I going to be sharing a room with a murderer, a car thief or a drug dealer? No, none of those feel right, she is too sweet. It has to be something smaller—maybe she's in for horse rustling, borrowing her neighbor's Sunday newspaper or fighting with her sister. Either way, I'm not going to be sleeping with my back to her, it never hurts for a girl to be too careful.

I have absolutely no idea what I'm up against being in a boot camp. If it were a church camp, we'd be playing games, singing songs and studying bible verses. Maybe not how I'd prefer to spend my summer, but I could handle it. Here at Camp ToughLove, I have my doubts we'll be singing songs at all. Instead, the warden will probably have us out in a field somewhere, digging holes in the hot sun. I sit up quickly, announcing to Stacia, "I hate digging holes."

The look I get is priceless. No doubt Stacia's now the one with serious concerns about the stability of her roommate. "Huh?" she asks eloquently.

"Holes," I explain. "I don't want to spend my last summer before high school digging holes for the sinister lady warden. I like the idea of getting a tan, but it'll totally destroy my nails."

Stacia is once again laughing uncontrollably—again most likely at my expense. I'm glad I can be a comfort to my horse-rustling roommate. "You are too funny," she says. "There's no warden, no holes and no criminals here. The kids are here because of issues they've had. Maybe they've suffered from depression, chemical abuse or have trouble relating to other kids. Parents send their kids here to better prepare them to face life's challenges. It's tough, but you will survive," she says with a smile.

Okay, I can handle this. No digging. No holes. No lady warden with rattlesnake venom in her fingernail polish. "So what do we do here?"

Stacia smiles broadly. "Are you sure you want to know? Wouldn't you prefer to be surprised?" I'm shaking my head, as I want to know what's coming. "Did you ever see one of those movies where somebody joins the army and they have to survive basic training? It's like that. There will be rope climbing, pushups, two mile runs, still more pushups and the occasional obstacle course. Other than physical training, we get some class work in science and English, and there is also a holdover from Camp Agape, a bible study. Mind, body and spirit, we get it all."

I'm nodding while I process this new information. Stacia continues,

"There will always be someone telling you what to do, when to do it and how to do it—and you've got to do it."

Five minutes later, I am outside on my cell phone calling my father. There is no way I am staying here. It's clearly a mistake I ended up here. The important thing to remember is my father talked about Camp Agape, not Camp ToughLove. His intention was that I would spend my summer there, learning about religion and things—not here with the troubled teens at a boot camp. Infuriatingly, the call goes immediately to his voice mail.

"Dad, it's me," I say, trying to sound as pathetic as possible. "There's been a mistake, a colossal mistake. Camp Agape ended last week and now I am trapped in a boot camp for wayward youth. Please call me back before I'm transformed into a bloodthirsty marine or murdered in my sleep by a troubled teen suffering from relationship issues. Please call soon."

Hanging up, I realize there's another way to fix this. The camp administration is set up at the University Center, one of the newer buildings on campus. I head there, confident my outrage at being enrolled at the wrong camp will elicit sympathy. It's not the first time I've been wrong.

"You've got to be kidding me," the sour-faced man says. "You've been left at the wrong camp? And I'm supposed to take your word for it? You wouldn't be the first to try to get out of the camp because it's too tough." He gives a dramatic pause before continuing. "In fact, I've been expecting someone to try to talk their way out of here." He opts not to steeple his fingers while saying this. What a wasted opportunity.

"I have your online registration right here," he says, pointing to his laptop screen. "Constantine Hill registered you on Monday for this camp. Our church camp ended last week, which he would have noticed when he completed the registration form. The only way to leave camp early is to have your father stop by, and only then can I release you to him. However, there are no refunds after camp has started."

I look at him, willing him to believe me, to help me escape this tragic mistake. "Please, I can't reach him. He's away on business and can't answer his phone. I know he'd want me to be happy and not here, suffering in the wrong camp." I try to give him my best puppy-dog look.

He's not budging. At all. "Our camp is named Camp ToughLove for a reason, Miss Hill. Parents want what is best for their children, even if it means enduring some short-term hardship to create a better, stronger child in the long run." He gives me what might pass for a smile in some shabby traveling carnival. "There is a bright side. A summer here will keep you out of juvenile detention in the future."

Some bright side. I've always been a glass half full kind of girl, but I don't see the brightness here at all.

6 | THE MALE OF THE SPECIES

Two figures shimmer in the twilight. I almost missed them—I'm preoccupied and they're down at the end of the hall. The day's last light shines through the entrance, illuminating their transparent nature. Their bodies have no mass, simple shadows playing tricks with the light. However, I'm drawn to them, knowing these are spirits here in our world. Walking steadily in their direction, I wonder why they are here. They have their backs to me, heads leaning in conspiratorially, having a conversation only they can hear.

I step up, curious to know what they're discussing. There are times when my curiosity has gotten me into trouble. This is one of those times.

A hood is thrown over my head, cutting off all light and air. It's sudden, it's vicious and there's nothing I can do about it. My hands beat without effect against the heavily corded muscles holding the hood in place. I'm frantic knowing I could die right here in this hallway.

Without any reason, my mom's face pops into my head and I'm able to force out a semblance of calm. I stop struggling, letting my arms slide off my attackers and after a moment, allow my knees to give out. I want my attacker to relax—let his guard down however briefly—so I can gain some advantage here.

With my attacker now forced to hold me up, I put all my weight on my right foot while I lunge back as hard as I can with my left. I want to wallop this guy and I might have only one opportunity. However, I miss, not connecting with anyone. Thrown off balance, I pitch to the floor. Clawing to get the hood off, my screams echo down the hallway as I realize there is no hood.

My gasps are now the only sound as my heaving lungs fight to replenish oxygen. Face planting into the gross carpet—some twenty years past its freshness date—leaves me sick to my stomach. The post-adrenaline shakes take me and I want to puke.

I roll over and there's no sign of an attacker, or a hood, or even a pair of ghostly visitors. It's just me and the half dozen people staring at me.

What just happened? I wish I knew. These paranormal experiences are usually sudden and powerful, and then wham-bam-gone, however this one has left me fearing for my safety here. There's something about this place that's dialed up my spookometer to well past normal. I can't help but look over my shoulder as I hurry down the hallway, anxious to be with other people—even if it's the troubled teens of Camp ToughLove.

Moving as a group, we head to the University Center for a gathering time after our dinner. I shuffle along with Stacia, as we bring up the rear. While not exactly an exciting dinner, the Sloppy Joes and greasy potato chips filled me up. What I found most interesting during dinner was watching the interpersonal dynamics of the other residents. Given the Camp ToughLove resident's supposed inability to cope with conflict and relationships, I thought it would be interesting to observe their behaviors. I began to feel like Jane Goodall as she observed the chimpanzees with nothing more than a notebook and pair of binoculars.

I quickly noticed the males' quest to be recognized as the dominant male. The posturing, the swagger, the glaring eyes. It wasn't long before I witnessed actual physical contact as a pair of large males crossed paths and bumped shoulders. Out here in the wild, there are no manners, no halfhearted mumblings of "excuse me." Both males continued on their chosen path, acting oblivious to the offered challenge. To show a reaction would be to show weakness. I saw none.

The females have their own social rituals. They tend to group in pods, where they scrutinize not only the stray individual females moving about, but also members of rival pods. I began to notice the most vocal females—the ones loudly expressing their derision of other females— would have the largest pods surrounding them. The correlation played itself out again and again throughout the course of our dinner hour. My hypothesis—which I intend to prove during my forced stay here—is that the less dominant females will group into these pods as they offer protection from the most scathing of female leaders. So far, the leaders have not demonstrated aggression toward their own members. However, continued observation may establish the evolving nature of these pods and show the females' perceived security can indeed be fleeting.

The most dominant female at Camp ToughLove is Carrie. Although her stature is small, her razor-sharp wit can bring the strongest to their knees. It's almost funny, the juxtaposition between her sweet smile and the words coming out of her mouth. I'll have to make every effort to avoid being on the receiving end of her fury. It may be difficult to believe, but I can keep a low profile. That's why I'm bringing up the rear as we enter the University Center. Our group spreads out while Stacia and I continue to the top floor of the Kinnickinnic River Theater. The large auditorium is where we will hold our evening gatherings. No singing around the campfire at this camp.

As we enter the empty theater from the back and start making our way down to the front, Stacia stops and grabs my arm. "Do you see that?" Her voice has an odd quality to it. Fear will do that to a person.

I look in the direction of her gaze. The two seats on the aisle in the front row are rocking. By themselves. No other seats are moving. I look at Stacia, whose raised eyebrows and wide eyes tell me a lot about her state of mind. She's terrified. I have no explanation for what I'm witnessing. However, I don't have explanations for most of the odd things happening around me. Some things just have to be accepted. "Come on," I say grabbing her hand and dragging her down the aisle.

We move deliberately toward the rocking seats, watching them as they continue to move, back and forth, back and forth. As we get closer, the rocking slows and stops altogether. Stacia peers around my shoulder staring at the seats, no doubt looking for a conventional explanation for the movement. There's no one hidden here, no wires attached and no air drafts that would cause these seats to rock by themselves. At the moment, the seats are deathly still, with not a sign of the animation we witnessed moments before. "I think we should sit here," I say as I gesture to the seats.

"Are you out of your mind?" Stacia asks with a hint of hysteria creeping into her voice.

"You'll be fine," I say as I sit, pulling her into the seat beside me. Stacia white-knuckles both of her armrests as though she is preparing to be launched on the Steel Venom roller coaster at Valley Fair. "Nothing can hurt you here," I reassure her, speaking in the most calming tones I can muster. "We are safe." It takes a few long moments before I hear Stacia let out the breath she had been holding. Her eyes dart around the room and apparently not spotting any immediate threats, her fingers relax, the color returning. Stacia's breathing evens out as the others take their seats nearby, the danger apparently over. She's going to have to get used to this sort of thing if she's going to hang out with me. Odd things just happen.

7 | HOOKED ON GHOST STORIES

Okay, I am surprised. There actually is a campfire here. After our evening gathering—really a thinly disguised lecture on personal responsibility by one of the counselors—we moved outside. The lecture was not at all relevant to me, however, as I am the responsible one in our family—I look out for both my father and myself. The talk was given by Ms. Neuman, an exotic looking woman dressed completely in black. She held the interest of the group, especially the boys—they followed her every move as she strode around the stage in her way-too-fashionable-for-camp heels. She said when we take responsibility, we admit we are the ones responsible for the choices we make. It's not other people or events that are responsible for the way we think and feel. It is our life, and we are in charge of it. Well, duh.

Our campfire is at Glenn Park, right across the Kinnie River. The interesting part was how we had to get across the river. I could feel the bridge bounce underneath as I walked across the old fashioned rope and plank swing bridge. The motion in the pit of my stomach was not really a feeling I enjoyed. But I kept my eye on the girl in front of me and was across before I knew it.

The night is warm and the mosquitoes haven't found us yet. The counselors direct us to sit on one of the 12 ginormous tree stumps encircling the campfire like a large clock face. I find myself sitting with Stacia on one side and a girl named Brooke on the other. Brooke has short blonde hair and cool–looking glasses, but she hasn't said a single word to anyone that I've seen. Is she just shy and reclusive, or possibly more of an angry loner? Who can tell when she won't say anything? Stacia and I look at each other, listening to the other girls talk.

"I've heard this place is haunted."

My head whips around. Haunted? Someone's speaking my language here. Two girls are huddled together, whispering.

"Yeah. Some of the girls have heard things. Voices, phantom basketball games, animals even."

"That doesn't surprise me. There is a slaughterhouse on campus, you know."

"No way."

"Way. River Falls is big into agriculture."

"Still weird, if you ask me."

"It gets weirder, though. One of the custodians was telling me that there used to be an empty house on campus. Apparently, homeless people were living in the attic. Somehow the building caught on fire and they were all trapped as the building burned to the ground, leaving them to die a horrible death."

"Tragic."

"I know. There's more. The custodian said there was a pool on campus paved over after a student drowned."

"That sounds like a rather extreme reaction."

"I know, right? I guess the circumstances were rather bizarre. The girl's roommate told school officials the drowned girl was hearing voices."

"Voices? Never a good thing."

"So true. The voices were getting increasingly insistent, demanding that she swim with them. Alone. At night."

"And she went? Epic."

"I know. There's still more."

"More? This place is giving me the shivers." I look down seeing my own goose bumps.

"A teacher hung himself just a few years ago."

"That stuff happens, right? It's unusual, but not really paranormal."

"This is. The custodian swears he was there and saw it."

"Saw what?"

"The body. It was swinging, as it hung from a rope tied to an exposed beam in a faculty house."

"So?"

"Don't you get it? They found the teacher's hanging body—some 12 hours after the deed was done—and the body continued to swing. The custodian said the campus police officer put his hand on the teacher, stopping the motion. However, the second he let go, the swinging motion started again. The campus police officer ran, leaving the custodian there by himself. The body swayed unrelentingly until the River Falls fire department cut it down. Two hours later."

"Epic. Truly epic." The two girls fall silent, lost in their thoughts. Stacia and I look at each other. I can only guess what she's thinking. We hold onto an uncomfortable silence waiting for something to happen.

It doesn't take long. Like most campfires that I've had the pleasure to sit around, someone starts to tell a ghost story and eventually the rest of the group joins in. There is an undeniable pleasure sitting in the light of the fire, listening to a scary story. You have no idea what lies waiting in the surrounding darkness, yet in the comfort of the fire, you want to hear tales that will make you squirm on the long walk back home. A girl is just finishing her story, telling us of a ghostly killer who was stalking teenagers, on a night just like this, in a camp just like this. When…

One of the boys jumps up behind us with a ghastly shriek. Many of the girls scream, several of the boys fall right off their benches, and the rest start to laugh as they realize the prank.

As the group settles down, Corey says, "I have one." The group quickly falls silent, as he stands up. "The reports had been on the radio all day, though she hadn't paid much attention to them. People were always escaping from jail, it seemed. The report said a crazy man had escaped from the state asylum. They were calling him the Hook Man since he had lost his right hand and had it replaced with a hook. He was a killer, and everyone in the area was warned to keep watch and report anything suspicious. But this didn't interest her. She was more worried about what to wear on her date."

Corey is prowling around the campfire as he tells his story. "After trying on several different outfits, she was finally ready and went outside to meet her boyfriend who had been waiting on the porch. They went to a drive-in movie with another couple, and afterward dropped them off and parked at the local lover's lane. She cuddled close to her boyfriend as they kissed to the sound of romantic music on the radio.

"Then the announcer came on and repeated the warning she had heard earlier. An insane killer with a hook in place of his right hand was loose in the area. Suddenly, the dark and moonless night didn't feel so romantic to her. The lover's lane was secluded and well off the beaten track. The perfect spot for a deranged madman to lurk." Corey says this directly to a pair of scared looking girls nearby. I can see them shiver.

Moving on, Corey continues. "Worried, the girl said 'Maybe we should get out of here,' pushing her boyfriend away. 'That Hook Man sounds dangerous.'

"'Aw, c'mon babe, it's nothing,' her boyfriend said, trying to get in another kiss. She pushed him away again.

"'No, really. We're all alone out here. I'm scared,' the girl said." Corey's impression of the girl's voice is comical.

He continues. "They argued for a moment. Then the car shook a bit, as if something…or someone…had touched it. She gave a shriek and said, "Get us out of here now!"

Corey is walking in our direction now. "'Jeez,' her boyfriend complained in disgust, but he turned the key and went roaring out of the lover's lane screeching his tires. They drove home in stony silence, and when they pulled into her driveway, he refused to help her out of the car. He was being so unreasonable, the girl fumed to herself while opening her door and stepping out into the driveway. Whirling around, she slammed the door as hard as she could. And then she screamed."

Corey was a large boy and his shadow throws much of our bench into darkness. He looks right at us as he speaks rapidly. "Her boyfriend leaped out of the car and caught her in his arms. 'What is it? What's wrong?' he shouted. Then he saw it. A bloody hook hung from the handle of the passenger-side door."

I hear one of the girls gasp. Most are quiet until Corey lets out a maniacal-type laugh and we applaud his performance. "Who's next?" he asks.

Everyone is looking around and Stacia elbows me. Hard. "Abbey has one." She nods at me.

I think she wants me to tell the story of what we heard today, but with a counselor here, I don't want to incriminate myself by saying I overheard it in an off-limits campus building. "Okay," I begin, "this happened in a little town in Ireland. It was a terribly dark night. The mother of all of rainstorms had set in and Paul was alone hitchhiking on the roadside. There were no cars on the road at all. The poor guy was not able to see beyond a foot due to the strong storm. Suddenly, he heard a car coming towards him. The car came into view and stopped close by. Wanting to get out of the terrible storm, Paul got into the car without thinking. He sat for a moment, catching his breath and looked around. Oh my God! There was nobody behind the wheel!"

I stand up, talking louder. "The car started to move slowly. Paul looked at the road and noticed a curve coming his way. Petrified, and still in shock, Paul began to pray for his life. Just before the car hit the curve, a hand appeared through a window and moved the steering wheel. Paul was almost paralyzed in terror as the ride went on, watching as the hand suddenly appeared every time the car approached a curve. At last, he somehow managed to open the door and jumped out of that horrible car. Without even looking back, he ran to the nearest town through the dreadful storm. When he reached the town, he was completely wet, exhausted and not able to utter a single word due to his state of shock. Paul was very shaken and went to a nearby bar, asking for two shots of Scotch."

I start moving slowly around the circle of stumps. "Still frightened and trembling, Paul started telling everyone in the bar about his horrifying experience. He told about the spooky car without a driver and the mystical hand that kept appearing. Everyone in the bar was frightened, realizing the guy was telling the truth." As I get to the top of the circle by the counselor, I stop and turn to face the group. Trying not to smile, I continue. "After half an hour, two guys entered the same bar. One said to the other, 'Hey, there's the guy who jumped into the car while we were pushing it.'"

My punch line is met with a number of groans. Thankful for any reaction, I find my seat next to Stacia. "Good one," she says.

"Time for bed," the counselor calls out. "Let's go." There's a general grumbling, but we get up and head for the dubious comfort of Grimm Hall.

Taking up our customary position at the back of the group, Stacia elbows me again. "Why didn't you tell them about the construction worker losing his hammer?"

"Why didn't you?" I throw back at her.

"Too shy," she says with a smirk. "Hey, do you believe in ghosts?"

I look at her for a long moment. "Yes, I do. When I was a child, one of my earliest memories was sitting on the couch, coloring next to my mother. I remember asking her, 'Who is that?' My mom would look around, not seeing anyone. She thought I was kidding and asked me who I saw. I told her, 'I see an old woman in the window. She has glasses and a funny white shirt where the collar goes way up on her neck.' My mom couldn't see the woman, but she said it sounded like my deceased great grandmother. I could see her plain as day, reflected in the window."

"Whoa," Stacia says. "Have you seen anything like that since?"

I pause, unsure how best to respond. "I see a lot of things," I reply, trying to be enigmatic. As a teenager, it goes against my nature to say or do anything to set me apart from everyone else. "But you see ghosts? Stacia asks.

I nod. "On occasion. I've simply learned, more or less, to accept these experiences as a part of my life."

We take the steps at the front entrance to Grimm Hall. The group dissolves as we head for our rooms, leaving Stacia and me alone. "You are a little unusual, aren't you?" Stacia says with a grin. She doesn't know the half of it.

8 | A NICE MORNING FOR THE RUNS

What a brutal morning.

Mr. Johnson has us running along the river just as dawn breaks. A certified night owl, I'm not much of a morning person. A typical morning for me involves a slow start as I move around, shuffling like some zombie-thing, picking up steam over the next hour and a half of my morning. After taking in equal amounts of breakfast and caffeine, a shower brings me to the edge of humanity and eventually, I feel ready to take on the challenges lying ahead. But no, that's not how my mornings will be here at camp. I'm startled out of a sweet dream, by what I believe to be a frying pan hammering on our door. With just enough time to throw on some shorts, a t-shirt and a pair of running shoes, Stacia and I are forced into the dim light of dawn to run for our lives.

It may not be that extreme, but he is yelling at us. Stacia and I quickly fall to the back of the bunch, as I gasp for air. Mr. Johnson is loudly condemning us for our apparent lack of effort. He may be used to being awake this early in the morning—when only the over-achieving birds are up getting their disgusting breakfast—but my body is rebelling. My mind is not awake enough to give my muscles direction, so my sleep-deprived body is left to flail on its own. Not a pretty sight, my gait is slow and awkward. This would-be drill instructor would be getting on my nerves—if my nerves were awake enough to resent his ranting. As it is, I do my best and keep putting one foot out in front of the other.

There's a point in the run that takes us along the edge of the woods overlooking the river. This is the section where our group gets spread out and I find I'm all alone as I keep a slow and steady pace. This is also the part that gets strange. I realize I'm near the woods, but the sounds… At first, it's the unusually loud crickets. The volume swells as nearly every insect within a quarter of a mile joins in. The birds start up too, many of them far away, giving a near-constant background of chirping. To add to the swelling nature choir, larger sounding birds begin to squawk intermittently.

My field of vision narrows, as the surrealistic nature of this experience heightens. The sheer volume of this event is unnerving. I'm able to continue the run, but only on autopilot. A nearby shrieking bird brings home the fact these are not Wisconsin birds. My gut—as well as my ears—tells me that I'm experiencing some sort of paranormal sensory shift. I've been transported far, far from Wisconsin.

Just as I'm expecting a jungle cat to step out, eyeing me up as a potential between meal snack, the experience comes to an end. The noise level drops from *turn-your-music-down-before-I-call-the-cops* to a volume more suited for a doctor's waiting room. I look around to see if anyone else heard it, but there's no one in sight. I think everyone's ahead of me. I shake my head and continue the run.

I am the last to return to Grimm Hall. Stacia had given up her attempt to help me stay near the group and finishes in the middle of the pack. Mr. Johnson—who is rapidly becoming my least favorite person—

stands with his arms folded across his chest. Looking at his face, I get the feeling he is not happy with me. And after he throws me under the bus, it doesn't take long for the rest of the group to join him. "Miss Hill needs a bit more conditioning it turns out. And since she can't run by herself, the lot of you need to join her. One more time gang, same course, but faster this time. Now go!" he barks.

I get a few shoves, and a few threats hissed at me as the group swarms past. This is so unfair. Still standing in place, I catch my breath, feeling the ache as each and every muscle in my legs complain in their own special way. Mr. Johnson steps into my space and leans into my face, "Miss Hill, you do not want to be last again. Go," he says with a menacing undercurrent in his tone. I'm not going to stay and argue with him, as much as he needs to be put into his place. Staying at the rear of the pack, as I strain to stay on my feet, I come to a realization. This camp isn't for me and I will do whatever it takes to get out of here.

I managed to finish the run in the middle of the pack. As we headed down the final stretch, four of the group slowed down greatly, allowing me to get into the middle. I felt a hand on my low back nudging me forward as well. And I don't believe for a second it was out of kindness, as self-preservation rules the day here. If I had to guess, I would say several of the smarter kids wanted me to stay out of last place so they wouldn't have to repeat the run again.

Walking to the University Center, I try calling my father again. Of course, it goes directly to voicemail. "It's me, Dad, still stuck at the prison camp. Please call as soon as you get this message. It's worse than you might think here. I heard some kids talking last night about an escaped killer almost catching this poor girl. Please call me before it happens again." Okay, I know I took things out of context, but they do it all the time on the news programs my father watches. And if there's one thing I'm good at, it's picking up on adult behaviors.

While I was on the second leg of my run, my oxygen-starved brain came up with a pretty good idea. If I can't get my father's help to escape my unjust incarceration, I am going to need the help of another adult. And I know just the person, remembering seeing a smiling face with the words, "I'm here to help you." His advertisement was on the dog-eared copy of the yellow pages sittingon the back corner of the information counter. I steer clear of the grumpy man who gave me absolutely no help yesterday. He's talking to another adult, no doubt discussing how they can be meaner to more kids, so I simply walk around the back side of the counter, grab the phone book and head over to the seating area.

Right here on the cover, among all the ambulance chasing attorneys, is the smiling face I remembered: Brian A. Thompson, attorney at law. "I'm here to help you." Nice and simple, no personal injury horror stories or promises of million dollar settlements. Just an offer to help. I decide right then and there, I want Brian Thompson, attorney at law, on my side. I dial his number.

"Brian Thompson." His voice sounds friendly enough.

"Mr. Thompson," I say trying to sound older than my years. "I need your help."

"I'm here to help you," he says, echoing his phone book advertisement. It makes me feel warm as I picture his smile. "What is the nature of your problem?"

"There's been a tragic mistake and I'm being held against my will."

"So you are being incarcerated?" He clearly has a sharp legal mind and I know I'll be sprung free in no time. "Are you in the Pierce or St. Croix County lockup?" he asks.

"Actually, neither. I'm being held at the River Falls campus."

"Ahhh," Brian Thompson drags out the word as he processes this left turn I've thrown at him.

"I'm at the boot camp here, Camp ToughLove. My father thought he was signing me up for the church camp—the church camp that ended last week. And now the staff here won't let me leave."

There is a palpable hesitation coming out loud and clear through the phone. Don't let me down, Brian Thompson, attorney at law. "Can I ask how old you are, Miss...?"

"Hill. It's Abbey Hill. And I'll be fifteen on my next birthday."

More hesitation. "Where are your parents? If it was your father's mistake, he should be able to help you."

My turn to hesitate. "I can't reach him. He's at a super-secret military base, doing research for a book. I've been leaving messages on his cell phone, but so far he hasn't called back."

"I see. How about your mother then?"

"She disappeared when I was 11. She went to Venezuela for work and just never came back." I don't want to talk about my mother with this stranger.

My mother, Katherine, worked as a doctor with the Doctors Without Borders organization, caring for the sick on basically what were extended mission trips. She went to troubled locations where civil wars and fighting occurred and though the doctors wouldn't take sides in armed conflicts, they were honor-bound to alert the public of abuses occurring beyond the headlines. Such candor had been known to raise ill will toward the doctors, often putting them further in harm's way. And though I could never accompany her, I was proud of her work and enjoyed the stories my mother would tell me upon her return.

The problem was when I was 11, my mother left for a trip to South America and never returned. A massive search was undertaken by the State Department, covering much of Venezuela, where she was last heard from. However, she had just disappeared— not leaving a single clue as to her whereabouts. My father flew down to conduct his own search after the State Department gave up. He returned empty handed and completely devastated. Life was never the same for us after that, as we both struggled greatly with her absence. A girl should not have to grow up without her mother.

"I see," he says again as I feel all hope fading away. "I don't suppose you have any relatives you can call on, do you?"

I'm shaking my head, which is so stupid because I'm on the phone. This was a bad idea. Thanks for nothing Brian Thompson, attorney at law. Then the first bit of luck I've had all week comes out of nowhere. "Miss Hill, why don't I meet with you in person? I could be there around lunchtime. There's a possibility I could do something to help. Let's meet and see what happens."

We make arrangements for my savior, Brian Thompson, attorney at law, to find me later. Maybe I am going to get out of here after all.

9 | BOW CHICKA WOW WOW

Lunchtime here is pretty much as it was back in elementary school. You get in line, with the weird combination of being hungry, yet dreading the muck the crabby lunch ladies are going to plop on to your still damp plastic tray. And since I skipped breakfast to make my call this morning, I am going to eat it—even if it's so gross I have to close my eyes. So I wait here, in the back of the line for my turn.

And then...

I smell the scent of a man. I hadn't even noticed someone stepping in front of me to grab some fruit, as I was so engrossed in my food options. His intoxicating fragrance pulls all thoughts away from food. My eyes take a stroll over the tall figure standing inches away. His damp dark hair, freshly showered, is worn long. A white t-shirt—snug in all the right places—shows off his broad shoulders, and his ripped jeans hold my attention longer than they should. He turns, forcing my gaze up. "Sorry to butt in," he says with a dazzling smile and steps out of line with banana and apple in hand. "I'm Turner. And you are...?"

"Abbey."

"Nice to see you," he says and is gone. I watch every step he takes as he gracefully maneuvers through the crowd. He must be new as I would have remembered someone so … memorable.

Bow chicka wow wow.

My cell phone picks that moment to ring. "Ahh," I answer. With my saliva glands overworked and my brain temporarily shut down, this is the only word I can muster.

"Miss Hill?"

I see a tall man waving at me from across the room. Brian Thompson is here. Carrying my lunch tray, I cross the room to meet with my new attorney. With a last glance in the new boy's direction, I am startled as he catches me staring. So much for my trademark subtleness. He smiles and holds my gaze for a moment. I almost walk into a trashcan, not exactly the impression I want to make. With as much grace as I can muster, I sidestep the obstacle and join my attorney, Brian Thompson.

Dressed casually for an attorney, wearing a tweed sport coat with elbow patches and khakis, Mr. Thompson has gray-flecked chestnut colored hair and a rather pleasant face that reminds me of a friendly uncle. He pulls a notebook from his worn leather briefcase, reaching across the table to shake my hand. "A pleasure to meet you, Miss Hill."

Still feeling rather flustered by the new boy, I force myself to focus as I shake my attorney's hand. "You too, Mr. Thompson."

Brian Thompson gives me a serious, yet compassionate look that he must use to great effect in the courtroom. "I am here to help you." No wonder that phrase is in his advertisement; he says it all the time. Getting directly to the point, he continues. "Having said that, I'm not entirely sure if I can help you. With you being a minor, the scope of my representation is quite limited."

"It's the fee, isn't it? I have some money."

He smiles a warm smile. "No, that's not it at all. It's just that …"

Brian Thompson hadn't actually stopped speaking, I have just stopped listening. I'm watching the new boy, who is sitting across the cafeteria, his head cocked at an angle looking around one of the alpha males sitting between us. And he's looking at me. The new boy is looking at me. Do I have something on my face? Did I spill my lunch on my t-shirt? No, my lunch is still sitting in its tray, untouched. The new boy arches an eyebrow, with an ever-so-slight nod to my attorney. He's asking me a question. I give him a shoulder shrug. The smile I get in return makes me feel all warm.

Brian Thompson, attorney at law, is looking at me. He's stopped talking and is waiting for me to respond. Sadly, I have no idea what he has asked me, so I wing it. "Yeah, that will be fine," I say nodding my head.

"Great," he says as he gets to his feet. "Let's go. It can't hurt to try."

I'm confused as I stand up, looking down at my untouched lunch. Oh well, there's always dinner. Dumping my tray, I follow my attorney out the door. Where are we going? Taking a last glance back at the new boy, I see he's still looking at me with those eyes of his. Hmmm.

"Miss Hill, where are the camp offices?" Mr. Thompson asks when we get outside. I point to the University Center, starting to get a clue. It may take a moment sometimes, but then I get up to speed pretty darn quick.

"My being here may seem unusual," Mr. Thompson begins as we walk in the afternoon sunshine, "but I have a teenage daughter who hasn't talked to me since her mother and I divorced. She wanted space and I let her have it. Lots of it. I was angry and pushed her away. Every day I regret letting my daughter go the way I did. You'll find as you get older it's the regrets that haunt you." He looked straight ahead with the air of a man wishing he were somewhere else. "So when you called, I knew I had to see if I could help you. I don't know if I can, but if there's one thing I'm good at, it's creating a stink."

The coming confrontation gets my heart pounding. It's going to be fun watching my vicious attorney take on the crabby camp administrator. In a cage match between the two, I'll put my money on the blood sucking attorney every time. After all, he went to law school to study intimidation and browbeating, right? We enter the lobby and there's an administrator behind the counter, waiting like an unsuspecting sheep. I follow my wolf across the lobby. Let the games begin.

"I'm Brian Thompson, attorney at law. I'm here to assist my client, Miss Hill." He gestures in my direction. Filled with pride, I find myself standing a little taller as I take in a deep breath. "Is there someplace we can talk?" Mr. Thompson asks.

The man points to the nearby seating area and we follow him. The man leans back in his chair, arms folded, clearly defiant. He doesn't offer a word, but just continues glaring at my attorney. I glance at Mr. Thompson, and he gives me a reassuring smile. "Miss Hill has been registered at the wrong camp. She does not have a criminal record in the juvenile court system and has been an exemplary student at her school." True, I do get good grades.

Leaning back, Brian Thompson, attorney at law continues. "Her father's intent was to register her for the Agape bible camp. A camp where she could get closer to God, study the bible and be an inspiration to her peers." Inspiration? That might be a little farfetched, but I'm okay with it.

"Miss Hill was not meant to be at this boot camp. Her father would want her to be at the right camp." That's what I said, only not nearly as persuasively.

"Mr. Thompson," the man starts, "our bible camp ended last week, so there isn't even an option to transfer her to another of our camps. Also, I have her online registration form, completed by Miss Hill's father, signing her up for this camp, Camp ToughLove." He pushes a printout across the table. Neither of us bothers to pick it up.

"Unless you can present one of her parents, I am not authorized to release her. As an attorney, you must realize the liability we could expose ourselves to if we released Miss Hill based solely on her word alone. Despite the good we bring to our camp attendees, most do not want to be here. Camp ToughLove is not an easy summer vacation playing video games and hanging out with friends. Our campers work hard to develop their character. Miss Hill would not be the first to attempt to leave our boot camp. Though I have to say she certainly has been the most creative in her attempt."

Mr. Thompson looks at me, the question implicit. I sigh. "My father is unreachable. And my mother has been missing for three years now. I have no other relatives I could call. Apparently, there's just me." Out of the corner of my eye, I see Turner, the new boy walking with our group, headed for the auditorium. My eyes track him until he is out of sight.

I stand up. "I guess I'll just have to stay here and make the best of it. I better run and catch up to my group." Turning back to Brian Thompson, attorney at law, I hold out my hand. "Thanks for trying. I'm glad you were here to help me." As I've seen a little ray of light in the camp, I am not going to fight my forced stay for now. No doubt leaving a pair of confused and relieved adults behind me, I turn to run after my group—and the new boy. Bow chicka wow wow.

10 | IT'S NOT EASY BEING GREEN

Stacia and I are headed for the Wyman Building to meet with our counselors. We are taking a shortcut through the long grass when I feel something gross under my bare feet. Something squishy. I grab Stacia's arm, pulling her to a stop. "What?" she asks.

"You don't feel it? It feels gross, sort of like mud, only slimier."

Stacia looks around as if she might break out running, but instead bends down. "Oh man," she moans. She is staring at something on the ground.

"What?" I ask. As I get no response, I squat down as well—and I am absolutely horrified.

There are dead frogs everywhere. Literally thousands of dead frogs litter the ground. I even have one sticking up between my toes. "Ughh," I gasp, lifting my foot. When I put it back down, I feel another frog squish underneath. Reflexively jerking my foot back up, I lose balance and put my foot back down harder, this time mashing a dead frog into the ground with my heel.

Stacia and I look at each other, totally grossed out beyond measure. Her coloring is going green and I know it's only a matter of seconds before she starts barfing. We have to get out of here, fast. I reach for her hand, desperate in my attempt to both comfort and be comforted. "No, don't look...down," I say as Stacia makes the mistake of looking down again. Horrified, she steps back quickly, pulling me off balance. Unbelievably things get worse—we topple over. Stacia lands on her back while I've landed on top of her. Stacia starts to scream and thrash. "No, stop!" I'm yelling as we roll over. The cold, slimy bodies of the dead frogs are pressing into my back, creating a panic I will never forget.

Remember on Halloween, when you were blindfolded and put your hand into cold spaghetti believing with all of your being that you were touching the intestines of some dead guy? This was far worse.

"Girls," a calming voice calls out across the field, stopping my scream before it leaves my throat. We are still thrashing, wrapped up in each other's arms, trying desperately not to be the one on the ground. Trying not to be the one touching the dead frog bodies. "Girls," the voice calls again.

We're still clutching onto each other but stop our struggling. "Help each other. Get to your feet and move this way." I give Stacia a push to help her get up. "That's it, now help her up, too," the woman instructs. Stacia reaches a hand down, and I see the terror haunting her eyes. Clutching onto her hand, I get to my feet. The frogs are still underneath my feet, but that is light-years better than having them touch my body.

"Move this way," the voice commands. I am finally able to look in her direction and see a woman with medium brown hair. Recognizing her as Mrs. Bies, the science teacher, I take a tentative step towards her. Stacia takes a small step forward, moans and stops.

I grab her by the hand and shout, "Run!" Together we sprint the 20 yards to the sidewalk, crashing into Mrs. Bies when we reach safety. Still freaked out beyond measure, I'm running my hands over my legs trying to get any frog remains off of my body. Stacia is bent over, heaving her guts up onto the sidewalk. I'm trying to catch my breath, wanting to push my panic as far away as I can. That was absolutely horrible.

"What killed all those frogs?" I ask Mrs. Bies. My voice sounds ragged, not at all like my normal voice. "I have never seen anything like that. It was so incredibly gross."

Stacia looks up, "I have to agree. Very gross." She spits out the last of her vomit as if to punctuate her point. I have to laugh, as there is nothing else I can do. Disgusting.

Mrs. Bies puts a hand on Stacia's shoulder. "I've studied biology for years and have never come across anything like this. I have read about mass wildlife deaths, typically near a polluted stream or pond. However, this is a university campus, not an industrial facility. We shouldn't be near any of the sort of chemicals which could cause a mass kill like this." She looks perplexed.

I have a question. "It's not just the killing that's odd, but is it normal for this many frogs to gather in a field like this? There have to be thousands here, and the nearest pond or river is a half-mile away. What would bring them here—just to kill them off? And it had to happen relatively fast, as I haven't seen a single dead frog beyond the bordering sidewalks."

Mrs. Bies looks around, a frown on her face. "I don't get it, but I'm going to make a few calls to search for answers. We have to make sure there aren't any contaminants on campus that could potentially harm the students. This is so odd," she says, shaking her head. "I hope you two are going to be okay."

I look over at Stacia, who is looking better—at least she has lost the green color. It wasn't her shade anyway.

At the Wyman Center, Stacia and I separate to meet with our counselors. Apparently, as a troubled teen, I need to meet regularly with a counselor to keep me on the right path. The right path? If they only knew. Not only do I stay on the right path, I own the path.

Ms. Neuman, the well-dressed counselor who spoke at our gathering on the subject of personal responsibility, turns out to be my counselor. Maybe I can learn some things about fashion from her, but if she is going to talk to me about personal responsibility, I've heard it. New subject, please.

I'm beckoned into an office and waved over to a chair across from Ms. Neuman. She sits back in her chair, crosses her legs and jots a note on a pad. I study her fashionable heels while she keeps me waiting. Finally, she looks up. "What would you like to talk about today, Abbey?"

Really, it's up to me? Okay, then. Dead frogs it is. "What's up with the dead frogs? Aren't frogs like a canary in a coal mine? You know, a low-tech early warning system that shouts, 'danger, danger.' Is this camp unsafe? Should I be worried? Do I need to call my lawyer?"

Based on the blank look Ms. Neuman is displaying, I would venture a guess this is not the direction she had been expecting. Can I help it if my mind is not wired like everyone else's? She rolls with it though and asks a follow-up question without hesitation. "If you could clarify, that would be most helpful. Is dead frogs a ghetto expression or are you referring to actual dead frogs?"

Ghetto expression? I live in Woodbury for heaven's sake. Our cheerleaders are named Buffy and Madison. We have a Trader Joe's and a Pier One. A soccer mom drives the only Escalade in the entire suburb. We are the polar opposite of ghetto. "Um, no. I'm talking real dead frogs, with real dead frog guts squishing between your toes. Stacia and I cut through the field outside and there were thousands of frogs lying there just dead. And they weren't no drive-by shooting victims, either." I used my best MTV gangster-sounding voice for the last line. Her look of irritation leads me to believe I may have crossed the line a wee bit. Oh well.

"I'll have maintenance look into it."

I was hoping for more of a rise out of her. "Is this place haunted?" I continue. "I've heard a few construction workers discussing some strange happenings here. It's more than dead frogs, isn't it? Are there ghosts in your camp?" That should do it.

Ms. Neuman puts down her notepad. She fixes me with a look of exasperation—a look I feel I've seen before. "I realize you're seeking attention here, Miss Hill. Many of the inner city kids are missing a parent, which would certainly justify your search for attention and validation."

Huh? Inner city?

"However, I have a professional responsibility to clear up your apparent misunderstanding. There are no such things as ghosts. The people who see ghosts are uneducated, delusional and weak minded. These are the same people who visit a psychic asking their dead Aunt Martha what numbers to play in the lottery. Abbey, just because the uneducated and street people surround you, doesn't mean you need to buy into their delusions. If you're ever going to rise above your current situation, you will need to have a sharp mind. If it doesn't make sense to you, reject it."

I already have. Standing up, I ask, "Where are you from, Ms. Neuman?"

Confusion written on her face, it takes a moment for her to answer. "I live in Stillwater. It's a charming little town located near..." I hold up a hand, stopping her in mid-sentence.

"I know where Stillwater is. I live in Woodbury, just two towns over from Stillwater. Woodbury is not the inner-city and it's not the ghetto. The only white trash we have is the newspapers on recycling day. I suggest you prepare a tad bit more before our next meeting." Maybe this counseling stuff works. I walk out feeling much better than when I arrived.

11 | GHOSTS OF GRANDMOTHERS PAST

"She doesn't believe in Santa Claus or the Easter Bunny. And I'm pretty sure she doesn't believe in the Pilgrims either." I'm telling Stacia about Ms. Neuman's refusal to believe in something she can't see. "People see ghosts all the time."

"All the time?"

"At least I see them all the time."

Stacia is looking at me warily. "You do?"

"Well, maybe not all the time," I backpedal. "But Ms. Neuman was way off base on a lot of things. She kept assuming I was from the ghetto. Stacia, are all you troubled teens from the inner city?"

Stacia's laughing. "Hardly. Us suburban kids have our issues too."

"Not me. I don't have any issues."

"Uh huh," she says, a grin on her face. "What color is the sky in your world?"

"Blue," I reply smugly. "Except it's a brighter blue than you're used to seeing. You should visit sometime."

Stacia is shaking her head. "And people say I'm the strange one in my family," she mutters.

We're walking through the first floor of Grimm Hall. "Brr, it feels cold right here," Stacia says to me. She has her arms wrapped around herself. I just shrug. "Didn't you feel that?" she asks.

"Yeah, it's a cold spot. I notice them all the time. Don't you?"

She stops and stares at me. "Abbey, that's not normal."

We have our science class with the only kind teacher here, Charlotte Bies. The classroom is located in one of the oldest buildings on campus, with creaking wooden steps, and a certain mustiness you'll never find in buildings built within the last 100 years. Sitting in the back of the room, I listen to her introduce the class. "Edwin Hubble said, that equipped with his five senses, man explores the universe around him and calls the adventure science. One of the most critical skills in science is that of observation. Most of the time we think of observation as something we do with our eyes; when we see something, we observe it."

Mrs. Bies walks down the center aisle, making eye contact with many of the students. "In fact, Yogi Berra famously said you could observe a lot just by watching. However, all five of our senses can be used to make observations: sight, hearing, taste, touch, and smell. And with those, we can make two kinds of observation: those that are facts, and those that are opinions. Facts are those things that are true for everybody. Opinions are beliefs based on personal preference. But that's just my opinion."

At last, a teacher with a sense of humor. So much better than Mr. Johnson and his rope climbing marathon in the gym.

Mrs. Bies has us close our eyes and hands each of us an object. After a moment, she takes back the object and has us jot down our observations of the object based solely on our sense of touch. Then with our eyes closed again, we are handed back the object to use our sense of hearing as we unwrap the object. Next, with our eyes open we use our sense of sight to observe the object. After making our notes we are told, "Now use your sense of smell to observe the object." Finally, Mrs. Bies asks us to place the object in our mouth and use our sense of taste to observe it. And just to be sure of my observations, I tasted two more. So far the thing I like most about science are the chocolate truffles.

After class, I wait for everyone to leave and then make my way up front to talk to Mrs. Bies. "Excuse me, Mrs. Bies," I tentatively begin.

"After what we've been through, call me Charlotte. How are you, Abbey?" She has a concerned look as she holds my gaze.

Reading my teenage paranoia, she quickly adds, "I meant, have you recovered from the trauma of the frog kill? That was horrible."

"Tell me about it. You didn't have frog guts between your toes. It was gross."

"I can only imagine. The Department of Natural Resources said they were sending someone out to investigate. I'll let you know what they discover. Though I can't imagine there would be any contaminates on campus which could be so deadly."

"Maybe it wasn't a contaminant." I'm just going to put it out there.

Charlotte pauses, one hand still in her briefcase. "Go on."

"There could have been another cause—a cause science doesn't recognize." I pause, taking a deep breath. "This camp is certainly an unusual place. Let me ask you this: have you encountered anything during your time here that has been out of the ordinary?"

Pulling her hand back out of the briefcase, Charlotte leans against the desk. She folds her arms, looking at me. "Besides 10,000 dead frogs?"

I nod. "Besides 10,000 dead frogs."

A sigh. Charlotte looks to be having an internal struggle. "I was working late two nights ago, logging some research time on a pet project. I live in an older house here on campus. I was alone upstairs with the door closed, no one else in the house. There are steps leading up to a small landing just outside my door. Unbelievably, at 12:15 a.m., I heard footsteps coming up those stairs. The doors downstairs were locked, no one should have been inside. Yet, I heard someone making their way upstairs. The footsteps stopped right outside my door. There was no place for the person to go, other than back down to the main floor. I call out, asking who's there. No answer was given, so I pulled open the door. Of course, no one was waiting there. I had clearly heard footsteps coming up the wooden stairs, so why hadn't I heard them retreat down the steps? I was determined to get to the bottom of things, and I searched the entire house. The doors were still locked— including the door chain—and no one was hiding inside the house. Believe me, I was quite thorough." She slowly shook her head. "I have no explanation for what happened, I just hope it doesn't happen again."

I hold Charlotte's gaze as I ask the hard question. "Do you believe in ghosts?"

"Science doesn't believe in ghosts."

"Nice try, but that doesn't answer the question. Do you believe in ghosts?"

"I am all about the science, so I can't separate my feelings and beliefs from what science offers: cold, reasoning facts. Ghosts are anecdotal. They are stories getting repeated over campfires, stories not amounting to anything more than what someone thought they saw."

As I know a few things about ghosts, I feel the need to set Charlotte straight. "But what about the sheer number of people who have seen…something? Ghosts, spirits, poltergeists, call them what you will, people are seeing these things. I've seen them." There, I've said it—no going back now. I've learned the hard way not to be so open when it comes to my ghostly experiences. Being ridiculed publicly as the spooky girl has taught me to keep my mouth shut.

Charlotte is nodding. "The thing is, almost everyone knows someone who has seen a ghost. The stories are everywhere, yet science doesn't believe. Science says there is no proof. Science looks for reproducible results that will either prove or disprove a hypothesis. And the trouble is, it's all random sightings, just anecdotal evidence. No one can prove there are ghosts."

I'm shaking my head. "I can."

Charlotte looks surprised. "You can?" Clearly not believing.

I nod and step toward the stairs, looking up the darkened staircase. "Edith," I call. I say nothing further and continue watching the staircase. Waiting.

Charlotte watches the stairs, her sense of expectation palpable. It begins with a creak—as if weight is being placed on the old wooden steps. It happens again, closer this time. Charlotte is straining to see into the shadows. I hear it again, the creak louder still. I feel Charlotte's hand touching my arm, though I keep my eyes on the stairwell. The sound is now right here. If I had closed my eyes, I would have sworn on a very tall stack of bibles someone had made their way down the staircase and was now in the room with us.

Charlotte looks around nervously as the wooden floorboards creak under the weight of … something neither of us can see. I feel a presence here.

It's difficult to explain what I'm feeling. It's a tingling, an energy that reminds me of the static electricity buildup I get when shuffling my feet on the carpet in the dry winter months. This ghostly presence doesn't scare me, however. The warmness I feel is more of a gentle stirring in my soul, bringing back the lush feeling of climbing into my grandma's lap when I was a little girl. It's funny, but briefly—two breathes at most—I smell grandma's perfume and recognize it instantly. Then sadly, it is gone. You know how old ladies have their favorite perfume? Grandma's was White Shoulders. It's a smell I will always remember.

Charlotte has to be feeling the presence as well—the hairs on her arm are standing up. "Who is Edith?" she asks. "You called out her name, and then…" Charlotte gives a little shiver. She has the deer-in-the-headlights look.

"Edith was my grandmother. She used to hold me in her lap and read me stories when I was a lot younger. I loved her more than anything." The thing is, I knew she was nearby. Call it intuition or some paranormal sense, but I could feel her. There are some things you just know, right?

"Are you telling me your dead grandmother was just in the room, here with us?"

"Well, maybe. I can't explain it, but the feeling reminded me of her. I just used her name and someone nice joined us. She had a familiar feeling, a comforting one. Just like being with my grandma."

Charlotte held up her hand. "I didn't see anyone."

"Neither did I." I held her gaze.

"But someone came down the stairs. I heard it. Someone was here with us, I could feel her." Charlotte paused. She had tears rolling down her cheeks. "And it was a her. I distinctly felt something feminine in the room with us. I wasn't scared. Okay, maybe a little at first, but once I sensed her, it felt oddly comforting. Was that a ghost, Abbey?"

I nod. "I've grown up with experiences like this all of my life. I've always wondered why some people have paranormal experiences while others don't. Over the years, I've learned I'm not likely to find those answers. I just knew she was upstairs, I could feel her. I knew I could summon her. You were talking about reproducible results. So what does this do for science?"

"I, for one, have become a believer. However, I'm concerned about you. Are you safe from the effects of this activity?" Charlotte frowns, worry flashing across her face. "Suppose it's you. What if you are the catalyst for this type of activity? Did the frog kill happen because of you?"

I'm shaking my head vigorously. "I'm normal. Or just about as normal as a 14-year-old teenager can be. Things just happen around me, that's all. You can't really believe I caused those frogs to die." I plead with Charlotte. I can feel my eyes threatening to tear. I do not want to cry.

She's shaking her head. "No, Abbey, I don't. You are a sweet girl. Not at all the sort of child to summon up an evil frog killing demon." She gives me a warm smile, making me feel better—at least until her smile is replaced by a frown.

"What?" I ask, following her stare. A blood-red symbol has appeared on the wall behind me. This symbol was not here earlier. It looks like a fancy lowercase letter F, except the top part is reversed.

While we stare at the symbol, a dot appears in the lower right, looking like this:

"What does it mean?" I ask.

Charlotte is shaking her head. "I'm not the one to ask. You should be asking Edith."

"I don't know if that was actually my grandmother. But I think it was."

"Do you know that for a fact?"

"No, I can't say it was my grandmother with 100 percent certainty. There aren't a lot of certainties where I'm concerned."

"That's for certain," Charlotte says with a smile. "I can't believe we are talking ghosts and facts within the same sentence."

I shrug. "Our world is a much bigger place than science believes. Did you know that when Shakespeare wrote, 'There are more things in heaven and earth, Horatio, than are dreamt of in your philosophy,' he was referring to a ghost?" Charlotte doesn't answer as we watch the symbol on the wall fade. The dot is the last part to disappear.

Obviously, there's a message here. The problem is, there are several things I don't know: who's sending the message and what does it mean? I just hope it's good news.

12 | AIN'T NO MOUNTAIN HIGH ENOUGH

I'm staring at the ceiling, not wanting to face the day. This place has taken a decidedly weird turn. And that is saying a lot coming from the princess of weird. Things happen to me that don't happen to ordinary people.

For example, something happened just a week or so before my mother disappeared. We had recently moved into an older farmhouse on the outer edge of Woodbury. After everyone had gone to bed, I was lying in mine, having trouble sleeping. The sound of footsteps moving down the hall made me sit up. As the footsteps got to my wide open door, my cat—who had been staring at the open door—got rigid and tense all of a sudden. She made a deep throaty hissing noise I had never heard her make before, her hair stood straight up and her cat nails were digging into my sheets. I reached to comfort her and she bolted from the room at my touch. After Lulu was gone, I had more time to process what had come in.

What I saw looked like a dark shade of black fog, however, I wouldn't describe it as a thick fog. It was hardly noticeable in the air except for the outlines of movement as it walked. I could see most clearly near its hips, distinctly making out legs as it walked across my room. It moved parallel to the end of my bed, to the corner where my closet was. I only saw the outline for probably ten seconds—though it felt much longer—but it was long enough to feel the full weight of what was in the room with me. Close to panic, a huge alarm bell was going off in my head. Shock took over me and all I could do was clench my teeth and sit anxiously while I continued to hear small noises coming from that part of the room. I had the feeling he did not want to be seen or acknowledged; he was simply trying to get out of his room after my parents had occupied it. I pulled the covers up, trying to hide. Eventually, I fell asleep.

The following night, I was about to fall asleep when I saw the tall, black transparent figure again walk through my door from the hallway. That's when I heard strange scratching noises on my wall from the corner. I had no doubt there was something there, but I didn't want to deal with it, possibly waking up my parents. Instead, I quietly crept out, went downstairs and curled up on the couch in front of the fireplace. In the morning, I went back to my room and looked at the wall. There were faint marks etched on my wall where I heard the scratching. Like most things I saw, I kept it to myself. I didn't want to be "that crazy girl." I wanted to be normal like everyone else. Except I'm not normal, and it is getting more and more difficult to hide that fact from the people around me.

Looking around the room, Stacia is already gone, and I better be moving too. Physical training awaits.

I join our group at the obstacle course. Mr. Johnson gives me a look as I step to the back of the line. All I can do is shrug. The group is ready to start the course, but Mr. Johnson holds up his hand stopping the first girl from starting. "Miss Hill, why don't you go first today?" Several responses come to mind, but I wisely keep them to myself. "Let me give you a warning: if you are too slow, the group will have to run the course a second time," he threatens. Groans erupt from the group. My reputation for speed precedes me.

Making my slow journey to the front of the line, I get several elbows along the way. I am clearly destined not to be popular. At the head of the line, Carrie gives me a look. "You better move your butt," she snarls. "I was supposed to lead the group today."

"There's always tomorrow," I tell her, trying to sound more flippant than I feel.

"Could you move any slower?" Carrie taunts.

"Whatever." Why is it that I always meet up with a mean girl no matter where I go? Life is never fair.

"Go," Mr. Johnson commands. I go.

I feel Carrie's hand on my back giving me a shove. Rather than propelling me, it causes me to stumble. I'm able to get my hands down, saving me from the embarrassment of a very public face plant. Getting to my feet, I push off as we race for the first obstacle, the tires. The tires are laid out in a grid pattern and I quickly figure out the secret is to take exaggerated steps, lifting my knees high like a country music dancer. It looks silly, but it works. I'm through just as Carrie is getting to the tires behind me. She's gaining on me quickly, though.

The tunnels are the next feature I get to endure. It looks as if they brought in sewer pipes for us to crawl through. The concrete is murder on my knees, so I crab walk my way down the tunnel. Carrie is right behind now. "Move," she shouts at me, the sound echoing down the tunnel.

Daylight is ahead and I'm out. A steep climbing wall is up next. The wall is wide enough for several of us to climb at the same time. Multiple ropes hang down to climb with. I cut off Carrie to grab the closest one. Just like gym class, I grip and pull, grip and pull. Glancing to my right, I see I'm actually moving up the rope faster than Carrie. This spikes my adrenaline and I become a machine, never tiring as I make my way up the wall.

At the top, I look over the side at the steep slide and I'm paralyzed. I hate heights. Carrie catches up and with little regard for her safety, throws herself over the edge. My hands are shaking. I just can't do it.

"Take my hand," a boy's voice offers. I look up to see Turner holding out his hand. "We'll go down together."

Numbly, I grab his hand and off we go. I give a shriek as we slide down the brushed metal surface, with little to none in the way of friction to slow us down. A pile of sand breaks our fall at the bottom. Not exactly a graceful landing, I pitch forward on my belly, landing hard.

Right by my outstretched hand I spot Carrie's glasses. She also had a hard landing and is on her hands and knees searching for her glasses— that are now in my hand. Turner is tugging me up by my other hand, encouraging me to continue.

"Hang on," I tell him. Looking to Carrie, I hold out her glasses. "Here they are." She looks at me for the briefest of moments, not saying a word and takes them from me. Clearly not overly sentimental, she is up and moving for the next obstacle without saying a word of thanks.

Whatever. Still holding Turner's hand, we race for the pylon obstacle. Imagine some very short telephone poles driven into the ground. At the obstacle's start, the pylons are placed low and close together. Once they are surrounded by a muddy bog, the pylons get higher and spread out—far enough that you no longer can step across, you have to jump from one to the other. To make things more difficult, the pylons are not in a straight line. They are arranged so you have to jump to your left, then to your right and then back to the left. The zig-zag pattern continues until the end. If you slip or miss your jump, a mud bath is your reward. Way too much fun to have before breakfast.

Turner gestures for me to step up on the first pylon. A glance to my right shows me Carrie is already onto her third pylon. I step up and move across the short distance to the next pylon. It's a bit more of a stretch to reach up to the third one. Not being the tallest girl, getting to the third pylon means a small jump up. Arms outstretched for balance, I hop up to the top of the pylon, which is just large enough for both my feet. Wobbly and fighting for balance, I size up my next leap.

This one is to my left, and a good foot higher and six inches further than the last. Feet together, I crouch and jump. My forward momentum almost takes me headfirst off the pylon. This near plunge teaches me I should be jumping with one foot at a time—sort of like crossing a creek by leaping from stone to stone.

The fifth pylon is to my right. I turn, orienting my body for the jump. This pylon follows the same pattern: a little higher and a little farther. Carrie is just beyond my pylon, still several ahead of me.

Carrie makes her leap, sticking her foot off the edge as she reaches toward her target and then pushes off with her back leg. Built like a soccer player, her legs look strong and her leaps require little of the effort that mine does. Though she doesn't exactly stick her landing, Carrie's balance is better than mine.

A question pops into my head. What would happen if I were to actually jump from post to post just like crossing a creek? Go big or not at all, right? I take a moment to size it up. Deep breath. Go! I jump to my right, landing on my right foot and then immediately jump to my left, landing on my left foot. So far so good. Pushing off, I repeat the process, again and again. It's working, I am now even with Carrie.

Glancing over at me, Carrie's look of determination—she clearly does not want to be beat—is totally evident on her face. Tough bananas. I jump off, finding my rhythm easily and start to pull ahead of her. I hear a four-letter word from Carrie, who's now in second place. Ah, satisfaction. My legs are beginning to feel like rubber as I see the end approach, but there are just two more pylons to go, then a longer jump off the last one to take me past the mud bog and a 20-yard sprint to the finish. I'm definitely going to beat her.

Several things happen as we grow up. Our body begins to mature and we get a little faster and a little stronger. Mentally, we are also maturing. We learn lessons from what life throws at us. In step with losing some of our childlike innocence, is the realization not all of life will go as we have planned. I did not beat Carrie.

Pausing on the last pylon, I size up my last—and longest—leap. I can do this. Deep breath in, I grunt loudly with the effort of my jump. My legs striding in mid-air, I land awkwardly and pitch to the side. I've got a mouthful of sand, as I seemed to have landed face first. Carrie jumps right after me, sticks her landing and races off for the finish line.

Determination lights my inner fire and I'm on my feet, spitting out sand, as I pump my arms attempting to catch up to her. I'm able to get close and make a last second dive as we get to the finish line. It's not enough though, as she beats me. However—and this is the important part—I was close. When I first got to camp, I never would have guessed I'd be able to keep up with someone like Carrie. I almost beat her. Even though my self-confidence soars, I'm still not ready to admit this camp might be a good thing. That is, until…

"That was impressive," Turner says, holding out a strong hand. He brings me to my feet effortlessly, my hand lingers in his, my eyes holding his. His smile is enough to bring my heart rate racing like I was right back on the obstacle course. Only this time, I'm right where I want to be.

13 | BAD GIRLS

"Science is my thing," Truly says on our way back from breakfast. She's wearing the same blue sweater I first saw her in. "In fact, I can tell you the three letter scientific term for hard water." My blank expression no doubt gives her license to continue.

Smiling, she says, "Ice." These French are so funny.

"I don't see much of you around camp. Where do you hang out?"

Shrugging, Truly says with a vague smile, "I've been around." Having read of the Cheshire cat's smile in *Alice in Wonderland*, I wonder if I am getting the whole story when I see Truly smile. I'm going to have to keep my eye on her. Never trust the French, I always say.

We go our separate ways as we enter Grimm Hall. A shower would be a good thing before lunch. The combination of sweat, dirt and sand would take away even the strongest of appetites. Besides, Turner should be there eating lunch too.

I head for the shower wanting to be done before Stacia comes back. My muscles are sore. As I stand under the hot stream of water, I'm stretching when it occurs to me that I can actually see some muscle. I straighten my arm and see the backside of my arm tighten up. I don't think that muscle was there before. Nice. I hold up my arms flexing my biceps. I may not be a plumber, but I sure got pipes.

A nearby giggle pulls me from my fantasy world. I'm thinking in the world of community showers, it may be best if I hold off on trying out my bodybuilder poses. It's just such a unique experience to finally see a muscle. I haven't always been the most active girl in the world. I grab my towel and look around to see the source of the giggle. Of course, it has to be Carrie. I hightail it out of there.

I feel a hand on my shoulder as I'm opening the door to my room. It's Stacia. "Where have you been?" I ask her.

"I ran into Truly and we got to talking," Stacia says, her eyes sliding down. "Nice towel, by the way." I'm wrapped in the tropical bird towel my mom had brought me from one of her South America trips.

"Yeah, thanks. I saw Truly as well. I always get the feeling that she's up to something."

"You never can tell with her," Stacia says. "She is a smart one. And you know how dangerous that can be." Laughing, she plops down on her bed.

I'm just about ready to make my bed, covers in hand, when I see it. The same symbol Charlotte and I saw last night has been traced into my sheet. It's as if someone had used a finger to draw the symbol right on my sheet. It's a delicate impression and the morning light hits it just right. I'm stunned. What does it mean?

"Stacia, come have a look at this."

She leans over my shoulder. "Look at what? Did you wet the bed?"

"Nice. Your mom must be so proud." I give Stacia an elbow. "What do you make of this?" I ask tracing my finger over the symbol on my bed sheet.

"I don't know what it is," she says. "Did you draw it?"

I'm shaking my head. "I found it this way. It's like someone drew it on my sheet. The odd thing is that it's the same symbol that Charlotte and I saw on the wall of her office last night. It was so strange, the mark faded away while we were looking at it. And then it was gone altogether."

"It's fading away here too." The line traced onto my sheet is beginning to disappear. "Our door was locked, wasn't it?" Stacia asks with a shudder. I nod.

Stacia folds her arms and looks at me. "Someone's trying to leave you a message, Abbey. Me, I prefer a hastily scrawled phone number every time. The odd symbol never really did it for me. It's too mysterious. The subtleness is lost on me—I'm a 'show me what you got' kind of girl."

"You are a big talker for a little twig of a girl, that's what I think. Besides, I have a feeling that the person responsible for the message is not in a place to receive my call." I give a dramatic pause. "If you know what I mean."

Stacia's arms are wrapped around herself, shuddering again. "Yeah, I think I know what you mean."

Lunch. The downside of my existence here. The food is worse than any greasy spoon truck stop that I've ever had the dubious pleasure of visiting. The atmosphere here is decidedly unfriendly, and the hostile looks I get remind me of a Survivor tribe sizing up their opponent right before they slam them to the ground and trample them in the latest reward challenge. I need to make some alliances here if I'm going to survive.

To make matters worse, getting to the cafeteria late means not having much of a choice where I want to sit. With all of the cliques, choosing the wrong table can be dangerous. I don't see either Stacia or Truly and I don't feel confident enough to approach Turner. So I'm standing in place with my tray, paralyzed with indecision. The pressure is far worse than I would have guessed.

"Excuse me," a voice says. My trance is broken by the boy appearing at my side. He's a tall boy with reddish blonde hair. Wearing a red shirt with Gunners written across his broad chest, he's dressed in athletic shorts and soccer cleats.

Nodding at the amazingly large pile of food on his tray, I say, "Clearly, you've never tried the food here. It's really quite awful."

The smile I get in return takes my breath away. "Let me ask you a quick question. How much does a polar bear weigh?" He doesn't wait for my answer. "Just enough to break the ice." He flashes a big grin and gives me an appraising look. "I like you, come join us for lunch."

Gently placing a hand on the small of my back, he guides me toward an empty table away from the rest of our camp. This is one smooth operator. I like him, even if he is a little cheesy.

I take the offered seat and he sits across from me. The rest of the table is quickly filled with his friends. "I'm Tommy," he offers. He holds my eye, a confident grin on his face. Most boys would be asking my name, or at the least, trying to fill the silence. Not this one.

I'm the first to give in. "My name is Abbey."

"A beautiful name." Without breaking eye contact, he grabs a carrot stick and takes a noisy bite.

"You are new here, aren't you?" I ask. "I didn't notice you here last week." Tommy and I are the only ones talking. The boys at the table are taking in our exchange, watching us while they eat. I have the feeling of being under a spotlight.

A nod. "Our soccer camp started today. It runs through Saturday. Six glorious days of fun in the sun. We're all staying at McMillan Hall and sharing this five-star dining experience with your camp." This gets a laugh from the other boys. "What about you, Abbey? What are you here for?"

He really should be asking what I'm *in* for. Honesty is best, right? "I'm here at Camp ToughLove."

Some of the other boys choke on their food. I get a raised eyebrow from Tommy. "Are you a bad girl, Abbey?" I don't appreciate the emphasis he gives to the word bad.

"Look, I was sent to the wrong camp. My father thought he was dropping me off at a church camp, and he's out on assignment and totally unreachable. So now I'm stuck here with the troubled teens in this haunted place." I may have said too much, judging by the looks I'm receiving.

"Haunted?" Tommy asks.

Biting my bottom lip, I nod.

"Really?" Tommy looks at me like I just reached over and helped myself to a handful of his mashed potatoes.

"It's okay if you don't believe me." I start to stand. "I should be going."

Tommy is out of his chair and to his feet in a heartbeat. "Abbey, please stay. Don't leave me here alone with this lot," gesturing to the other boys at the table. "For what it's worth, I believe you." I look into his eyes, seeing only sincerity. I sit.

"Can I see your cell phone?" he asks.

I slide it over, unsure of what he's up to. What I am enjoying here, is the fact that he is up to something—and I'm the center of his attention. It reminds me of what I've been missing since my father left. What a girl finds so special about her father is that she's the focus of his loving attention. A girl knows her father is interested in everything about her and most importantly, he isn't judging. My father loves me for all my quirks, all my faults and even all my bad fashion choices. I wish he were here. Why am I sitting here in front of this über-confident boy, fighting back tears as I think of my father?

Tommy holds up my phone and takes a picture of himself. He slides it back. "I added my number, so call anytime. If you need something, call me. Be it hauntings or ghosts, I might be able to help." He leans back, with a smile so supremely confident, I just have to laugh.

"All right. I'll call—if I need your help. I sincerely appreciate your offer, but I should be running." I stand and take the long walk across the room, knowing his eyes are following me. My smile betrays me by showing my pleasure at his attention. Things are looking up here at Camp ToughLove.

14 | DON'T MAKE ME RELEASE THE FLYING MONKEYS

Sitting in my bible study class, listening as the teacher talks about the Holy Spirit gets me thinking. What would he say about the spirits I see? Would he understand? Would he have some special insight as to why they reach out to me? After class, I decide to test the spiritual waters.

"Excuse me, Mr. Kindle. I was wondering about ghosts. Where do they fit in with theology?"

Mr. Kindle is a short man stuffed into a too small tweed sport coat with sleeves that are way too long. He appears to be going for the academic look with his cool guy glasses and his hair worn stylishly long. His loafers even have the prerequisite tassels.

Mr. Kindle gives me a thoughtful look as he processes my question. "Well, they do not teach you about these sorts of questions in theological college. In fact, Christian theology is embarrassingly silent on the matter of ghosts. There are reasons for this. Contemporary Christian theology eschews dualisms of the soul and body. Christ, as represented in his resurrection appearances, remains embodied, not free-floating ectoplasm. The perceived wisdom about ghosts is that they are eternal souls wandering on the other side of death, free from their bodies. So the theological difficulties with ghosts become evident. It's not that theologians dismiss the mysterious and inexplicable in the natural; take angels, and the miracle of the virgin birth or the raising of Lazarus as examples. But ghosts—detached, ethereal, grief-stricken souls—do not find an easy place in this Christian theological account of the creation."

Mr. Kindle looks at me as if he is seeing me for the first time. "Why are you asking about ghosts?"

I'm not entirely confident that I should be sharing this, but I'm worried there's a special place in hell for those who lie to their bible study teachers. "Ghosts have been reaching out to me. But I'm not quite sure what they want. I believe they are trying to tell me something. Have you come across this before?"

Mr. Kindle shakes his head, weariness evident in his manner. He sits down on the desk. "This is not uncommon, you know. Children are seen and heard, some are even singing. Favorite aunts, uncles or even parents, are seen—usually coming to comfort those they leave behind. It is assumed, even by believers, this is proof ghosts are spirits of dead people and most mean us no harm." Arms folded across his chest, his voice creeps up in volume as his passion grows. "This is a great error, for all ghosts, without exception, are demons. They are wicked angels, followers of Satan whose only task on this earth is to deceive and to harm. Demons are like stalking lions, watching for easy prey. And when they find someone, they pounce with a ferocity that is boundless and utterly vicious. Demons are not just forces—they are real creatures. Under normal circumstances, they can't be seen, but they can assume human likeness whenever they wish. This is how a friend or a favorite aunt can suddenly appear to you. Demons know what they look like, what they sound like and everything about their histories, right down to their pet names for you. So, they mimic them."

Mr. Kindle is getting louder, a notch or so away from yelling at me. He gestures emphatically with his index finger. "There is evil in our world. The Bible says Satan was banished by God to just one place. You know where that place was? Earth. If you don't believe me, just watch CNN for 20 minutes. Ghosts are never friendly, Miss Hill. They are always wicked, even if they appear to be kind. Their purpose is to make us believe they are spirits of the dead. Once they manage to delude us, they continue to hold our attention, so any belief we may have in God as presented in scripture, is eroded to nothing. We are warned of this in scripture. We are told no man has ever returned from the dead, except for Jesus Christ and those he raised from the dead as special miracles."

On his feet now, Mr. Kindle moves into my space. There is a definite menace in his voice. "This is not a path you should be treading on Miss Hill. There is no place for these spirits in Christianity. And truth be told, I'm not entirely sure there is a place for you in my class."

Clearly dismissed, he turns his back on me. With tears running down my cheeks, I run from the room.

Turner is the one who finds me.

I'm sitting on the front steps of the Wyman building. Seriously late for my counseling appointment, I can't face Ms. Neuman right now. Why does life have to be so difficult? I know life will always throw things at you, some good, and some bad. My father taught me how we mature is based on our responses to these challenges. I am and always have been the stereotypical optimist, never missing the upside to any of the bad things that inevitably come my way. But—and this is an enormous but—why does this camp have to be so supremely unfair?

"You look as if someone just took your last cookie." Turner sits down, leaning back and looking into the distance, the epitome of cool. "My father used to say if life hands you a lemon, make lemonade. But if it hands you a pickle, you should just give up—because pickle-ade is disgusting."

Okay, not the cliché I was expecting. I have to fight back a smile. I do not want to smile right now.

Turner is not one to give up, though. "Hey, my life sometimes sucks too. So much so that my ears pop just thinking about it."

I'm trying not to smile, as I wallow in self-pity, feeling sorry for myself. Doesn't he get that? Instead, he gets my elbow.

Laughing, Turner says, "I'm happy I can help. You looked like you needed something."

Looking at Turner, his eyes are a place where I can get seriously lost. "Thank you."

I get to my feet, a sigh escaping. "I better go see my counselor. She is probably thinking I'm off stealing the wheels off of abandoned ghetto cruisers in my hood."

"You are one strange girl," he says with a smile.

I smile right back. "People keep telling me that."

"Tell me about your mother, Abbey."

Again, not what I was expecting today. Ms. Neuman had been waiting for me outside of her office. Always the vogue dresser, she has on high heel boots, jeans, black shirt and a baseball cap. I'm waved into the office, where I curl my legs underneath me as I sit across from Ms. Neuman. I don't say anything as I watch her watching me. Let the derogatory comments begin.

"Tell me about your mother, Abbey."

"My mother?" I ask, stalling for time. Ms. Neuman's face doesn't give away anything.

She nods, holding up a file folder. "I took your advice from our last meeting. My experience has been that with inner...uhh... disadvantaged youth, typically the issues stem from an absent parent. As I said, I did prepare for this meeting. What I found was that you have an absent parent."

"I wouldn't say she was absent." I don't want to be having this conversation—and especially not with the insensitive Ms. Neuman. "You make it sound like she has been missing school."

She is shaking her head. "I'm not implying anything, Miss Hill. I'm just asking. Please tell me about your mother." Her earnest gaze makes my decision for me.

"She was a beautiful lady, so full of life. I miss her. We used to be very close. I think our time together was so precious for each of us because she was gone for weeks or months at a time. My mother was a doctor and frequently traveled with the Doctors Without Borders organization. I learned so much from the stories she would tell when she came home from each new exotic place. Every trip would mean a souvenir—not touristy stuff, but something handmade given to her by a patient's family. I have a wall filled with things from places like Haiti,

Peru, Rwanda, Colombia, Afghanistan, the Ivory Coast and Venezuela."

"I would often sit with her on the couch, my feet draped over her lap, and we would talk about nearly everything. Her experiences would help us process the events of my day. She had such a unique perspective on life. Mom had an energy about her that burned so brilliantly. I believe that was one of the things that made her so successful in her travels. People were drawn to her, and even though my mom often couldn't speak their language, it didn't hurt her ability to communicate with them."

Ms. Neuman held my gaze. "What happened to your mother, Abbey?"

"Her name was Katherine," I begin. I hate this part. You see, I don't know if I should be saying was or is. I don't know if she is alive or… "All I know is she went to Venezuela and never came back. She had been down there for a little over a week of her three-week stay and was traveling through a remote area. She never made it to her destination. The State Department conducted a search, though they came up completely empty handed. She was just gone. We couldn't accept that she wasn't coming back home. My father went down to South America with a friend and I guess they were quite thorough, even paying off local officials. Yet, the result was the same."

My tears are warm on my cheek. I don't care if I am crying in front of this woman. I miss my mom.

I'm not sure how it happened, but I feel her arms around me. It may have been the briefest of moments, it may have been several minutes, but the comfort felt … nice. Don't get me wrong, though, I still don't like this cold-hearted witch.

Awkwardly disengaging, I can't help but think how much I want this camp to be over. I really want to go home. I don't believe it's asking too much to have a kindly man step out from behind the curtain and say to me, "Close your eyes and tap your heels together three times. And think to yourself, there's no place like home."

15 | SIGN, SIGN, EVERYWHERE A SIGN

It's the oddest thing. I'm sitting in the cafeteria, generally ignoring the vegetables on my plate. The meatloaf and mashed potatoes are okay, but I don't want to eat the peas. I mean, who really likes peas? Outside of senior citizens like my grandmother, I don't know of anyone who actually enjoys the pasty feeling of peas when they squish in your mouth. I'm sitting with Truly and Kirsten at the dinner table, all the while keeping an eye on Turner, who is sitting two tables over and Tommy, who is across the room sitting with his loud soccer buddies. I catch both of them looking at me. Interesting.

Some people believe the essence of happiness is having choices available to you. Others see choices as a series of paths, living with the fear of taking the wrong path, leading to heartache and catastrophe. I'd imagine these people often become quite indecisive. I look at choice as an opportunity to test the waters, discover which flavor I prefer. My favorite ice cream shop lets me try spoonful after spoonful before I decide. And that is how life should be.

"Abbey, are you even listening to us?" I glance over to Kirsten. No, while I heard their voices, I was not listening to what was being said.

"Sorry, I was a bit distracted." Not really feeling like volunteering an explanation, I simply give a nod toward Tommy.

"I can see why," Truly says, giving Tommy a look over. He smiles and stands up, obviously reading her attention as an invitation to visit our table. "Oh, he's coming over. What a charming gentleman he is."

"Hi, Abbey," a voice says to my side. A quick glance shows me it's Turner. The only problem with trying several flavors at the ice cream shop is that you don't want to intermingle more than one flavor. Not all flavors go well together. In fact, mixing flavors can be a very bad thing.

I watch Tommy confidently making his way across the cafeteria. This could get ugly. Turner is leaning on the table waiting for my undivided attention. I give it to him. "Turner. What are you doing? Don't you hate these peas? I know I do." Good God, I am babbling like a complete idiot.

"Hi, Abbey. Hi, girls," Tommy says holding each of our gazes for a long moment. He pauses when he gets to Turner. The two boys lock eyes, sizing each other up. Tommy is all about posturing as he inflates his chest, pulling his shoulders back. Turner's dark eyes have an intensity to them as he responds to Tommy's not-so-subtle dominant male of the species display. There's menace in Turner's eyes.

"Are you a footballer then?" Truly asks of Tommy. "You look like a striker if I had to venture a guess." She smiles at Tommy, and I'm almost sure she's batting her eyes at him. At this point, I will take any diversion to break up the tension. "So, do you like to score?" she asks.

Well, almost any diversion. Her last comment makes me want to bang my head on the table—I am embarrassed enough for the both of us. Luckily, Tommy doesn't appear to catch the double meaning. "I do play striker, how did you know?" Tommy grabs a chair, spinning it around and sits across from Truly. Arms folded across the chair back, he smiles at Truly, waiting for her answer.

This is my opportunity to further diffuse the ticking time bomb otherwise known as my life. "Can I talk to you?" I ask Turner, grabbing his arm, wanting to move him away from Tommy.

I start to stand and everything comes to a screeching halt.

My plate. My peas. My breath catches in my throat as I look down. The symbol is back, this time arranged on my plate using my untouched peas. What does it mean? I glance toward Tommy and Kirsten, but they haven't noticed. Truly is looking at me with an odd expression on her face, no doubt considering the possibility that I am having an aneurysm right here in the cafeteria.

Time to leave. Pulling Turner's arm, I drag him away from the table. He allows himself to be led by me and we make our way outside. When we pause under the large oak shading the entrance, he looks at me and says, "What was that about?"

"What was what about?" I can play dumb when I need to. And I really need to at the moment. My mind is still racing. I am clearly on the receiving end of a message, but I have absolutely no idea what it means. The symbol doesn't look at all familiar. Why would that particular symbol keep showing up when it doesn't convey any meaning to me whatsoever? And the other half of the question: Who? Who is trying to communicate with me? I know I am not like other girls. I see a lot of strange things other people can't. I can sense when there is a presence—ghosts, spirits, whatever—nearby. This has always been my reality.

"Abbey?" Turner is looking at me with those eyes of his.

"Yes?"

"Are you alright? You looked as if you saw a ghost back there." His concern makes me feel better.

"Did you see my plate?" Turner has a quizzical look, so I try to clarify. "My peas, to be more precise."

"That is a lot clearer. Thank you." His sarcasm is not lost on me. I am and always have been, the master of the obvious.

I take a deep breath. "For the last several days, a symbol has been appearing around me. It showed up on the wall of Charlotte's—Mrs. Bies'—office and faded from sight before our eyes. The next morning I saw the symbol traced onto my bed sheet. And just now, my peas were arranged into the same symbol. I don't know who—or what—is trying to communicate with me."

I hate this part. In the past when I've shared some of what goes on in my life, I don't always get the response I was hoping for. Most of the time people don't believe me, or they think I am kidding. If I persist, the look becomes one of concern as they begin to mentally question my sanity. To tell the truth, at this point I usually just let them off the hook. I'll smile and say I was kidding. My past is littered with friends who didn't believe, friends I couldn't confide in and others that I wished could have been a friend, but I just couldn't risk the hurt. I can't remember the last time I had a close friend.

Don't get me wrong. This isn't a pity party. My life is not a sad thing—actually quite the opposite. I am secure enough to realize my differences are worth celebrating. And my lack of friendships has brought me closer to my dad, which in turn has led to worldwide travels and adventure. Not a bad life for a 14-year-old girl from Minnesota.

Turner is looking at me. I know the expression written on his face. I've seen it too many times. "Peas? Really?" He looks back at the entrance. "Hang on," he says. Turner disappears through the door, leaving me to wonder what he's up to.

In a moment, he's back. Turner's expression has changed, but I'm not able to read him well enough to see where this is going. He holds up his cell phone. On screen is a close up of my plate, the arranged peas clearly evident. "And you didn't do this?" I suspect he had known the answer before he asked. My father would call it doing his due diligence. You have to rule out the most likely scenarios before you can consider the most extreme options.

I shake my head.

"Have odd things like this happened to you before you came here?"

I nod. "Odd things yes. Odd things like these symbols, no."

"Give me an example, if you would."

Sigh. "As a young girl, I would spend the weekend at my great grandmother's house with my cousin. She would have Sally and I sleep up in the attic bedroom, a large spooky room where the wind would howl at night. She would tuck us in and turn the lights off, leaving us with only the glow from the outside streetlights to see. Every night after we were in bed, we'd be lying there trying to sleep as we listened to the wind and the creaks all old houses seem to have. Most nights, a figure would emerge from the large closet located on the far wall, the darkest part of the room. It was always the same: an older woman dressed in flowing white would step silently into the room. She had a gaunt face, a face that had seen a lot of hard times. It was a face that looked as if the tragedies of life had made their mark, leaving her bitter and resentful. This apparition would hold out her arm, pointing at us accusingly, a silent scream evident from her open mouthed expression. I have to tell you, it was a horrifying sight for two young girls to witness."

Turner touched me on the arm, a gentle gesture reassuring me far more than words ever could. "What did you do?"

"Sally would scream for my great grandmother. But you see, my great grandmother was an old school woman who didn't have patience for the games little girls play. The first time this happened, she came running up the stairs, the sound of her wooden shoes sounding like hammer blows on the steps. Of course, there wasn't anything in the room when she got there. The old woman figure sort of faded from view as soon as my great grandmother hurried up the stairs."

I shake my head at the memory. "It's not like that was the first time I've seen something unusual. Sure, I was scared, but nowhere near as terrified as Sally was. I remember holding her, feeling her body shake with fear and adrenaline. It took her a long time to settle down. It happened the next night, just the same as the first. Only my great grandmother didn't come running. It was bad. Sally completely lost it and sort of went away for a while. She never visited there again. And her family moved to another state several months later."

Turner shakes his head. "Intense. Do you believe this symbol is some sort of sign?"

I nod. "Yes, but I don't have a clue what it means. If I'm supposed to do something based on that symbol, well, it's not going to happen until they give me something more to work with. I sincerely hope lives are not hanging in the balance waiting for me."

Turner held my gaze, as I wonder what he's thinking. His hesitation brings instant regret on my over-sharing. "I'm not sure if I can help with the paranormal stuff, but I will have your back. If that helps…"

I'm fighting back my tears, unable to voice a response. All I can offer in return is a nod. Years of loneliness can do that to a girl.

I get the smoldering eyes again as he helps me to my feet. "I can't say I've ever met anyone quite like you, Abbey."

Doubt sets in as I'm walking back to Grimm Hall and I'm desperately hoping Turner's remark was meant as a positive.

16 | NINJA TURTLES ON SPEED

A shocking discovery today.

Alone in my room, I'm working through the day's events. Lying on my bed and staring at the ceiling, I'm pondering what it all means like some long-dead Greek philosopher. And it's not the underlying meaning of life I'm referring to here. It's that damn symbol—pardon my French. But I'm seriously concerned my brain may explode if I don't figure out the answer soon.

Frustrated, I roll over facing Stacia's half of the room. It takes a moment, but then it hits me faster than a ninja turtle on speed. I'm looking at Stacia's backpack. Off my bed, I'm across the room in a heartbeat pulling a blue sweater—the exact powder blue sweater Truly wears—out of Stacia's backpack. Stunned, I'm left with a big question: Are Stacia and Truly the same person?

Ms. Neuman waves me into her office. I'm not exactly sure how I feel about being here after my last visit. Talking about my mother brought up a lot of feelings hidden away for a long time. I still feel rather raw—if that's the correct word—after talking about my mom again. I'd almost rather spend an hour discussing my life in the ghetto instead. Almost.

Taking my usual seat, we sit quietly, each of us enjoying the awkward silence. I find myself once again taking stock of what Ms. Neuman is wearing. She has on a gray lace top, pinstriped slacks and gray and black snakeskin pumps. If nothing else, she's taught me the importance of accessorizing. As far as her counseling, it's like a shop teacher with missing fingers, you don't exactly trust the safety message.

Her eyes coolly study me, no emotion evident. I think she is waiting for me to initiate the conversation. Well, I have some news for her. She will be waiting a long freakin' time.

Two long minutes later, I begin to realize she is quite good at this. I fidget and start looking around the room, as I can't hold her gaze. I study the book titles, not finding anything interesting. Time is moving slower and slower, the silence feeling impossibly loud. I can't take it. She wins.

"So," I venture.

Her eyebrow rises, but she holds her silence. She is really good at this.

"What have you been up to?" I ask Ms. Neuman. "Been having a good summer?" I'll keep this light and impersonal. No more tears for me.

Leaning back and reaching for something, Ms. Neuman says, "What have I been up to? Funny thing you should ask. I was off campus last night and stopped by a bookstore. Barnes and Noble has a great selection of books. Their geography section is second to none." She has a book in her hands, which she hands to me.

Tentatively, I accept the offered book. Turning it over, the title takes my breath away. *The CIA's Guidebook to Venezuela.* The back cover copy reads, *This authoritative book offers a comprehensive assessment of contemporary Venezuela. Highlighting the need to avoid simplistic assessments of the past and present, it offers a clear-eyed understanding of Venezuelan reality today. This groundbreaking book details the true story of the CIA and US Coast Guard's secret mission to overthrow the Venezuelan government to gain control of the country's oil. Also discussed are the dangers for both locals and outsiders in the notorious badlands of the Guajira Peninsula on the Venezuela-Colombia border. Chock full of the latest Google Earth images, and on the ground accounts by CIA operatives, you will experience a Venezuela like few others have.*

Interesting.

"I thought it would make sense for you to learn more about the land and people that meant so much to your mother that she would be willing to risk her life for them. The book is yours to keep, Abbey. Let's cut our session short tonight so you can look through the book. We'll spend a little more time together tomorrow if that's alright with you."

Nodding, I let her escort me to the door and that was that.

Walking back to the dorm, I'm debating what to do about Stacia and her fake sister, Truly. I get the feeling Stacia has been playing both parts. Not wanting to confront Stacia, and have her deny the Truly hoax, I need a plan. One that would make it evident that her hoax is just that. Holding her blue sweater, I decide to tuck it back in her backpack where I first found it. Better to keep my newfound knowledge to myself for right now. For some reason, it's comforting to know that I'm not the only strange one around here.

17 | ONE MYSTERY SOLVED…

I am a stalker. As cat-like as possible, I have been following Stacia around camp. Wherever she goes, I am her shadow. It had taken a day and a half before I witnessed Stacia going into the bathroom and moments later, there's Truly coming out. It is funny that now I'm looking for it, I see Truly always wearing the same oversized powder blue sweater. Her hair is worn in a casual up-do, while Stacia wears her straight hair down. Truly has glasses, while Stacia doesn't—which I'm sure has just plain glass for lenses. Add the French accent and Stacia is magically transformed into the far more intelligent girl from France, Truly. This is a disguise truly worthy of Clark Kent. How Lois Lane never noticed the similarity is beyond me.

Watching my prey from around a pillar at the University Center, I almost blow my cover when a hand touches my shoulder. Expecting— and truth be told, hoping—it to be Turner, I am surprised to find Mr. Kindle when I turn around. "Miss Hill," he begins a little too loud for my tastes.

Since Mr. Kindle is the man who yelled at me the last time we spoke, I'm ready to give him a few things to think about. However, this is not the time or place to resume our previous argument—I just want him to go away. Quietly.

"About our discussion the other day, I have been giving it further consideration. I believe, as most enlightened Christians should, we must allow for the freedom of God to use people—both living and dead—for his good purposes. This is his world, after all. God set up the physical and moral laws, and he rules over these in love. When something is needed for his children, he spares no expense." Slipping off his glasses, Mr. Kindle wipes them on a white handkerchief pulled from his breast pocket.

"Really?" I ask.

He smiles a fatherly smile. "Really. I happened along a C.S. Lewis anecdote that was quite persuasive. Apparently moments after his death at Cambridge, C.S. Lewis appeared in the Oxford bedroom of J.B. Phillips, a dear friend of his, the man who translated the Bible in the Phillips translation. At the time, Phillips was in a deep depression that threatened his life. He refused to leave his chambers, refused proper food or exercise, and seriously questioned the love and election of God in his life. A 'healthy Lewis, hearty and glowing' as Phillips was later to record, stood before him, entering his room through closed doors."

I take a quick glance around the pillar to see Stacia still talking with a group of girls. Mr. Kindle pauses as he's wiping his glasses. "In this vision, Lewis spoke only one sentence to Phillips: 'J.B., it's not as hard as you think.' One solitary sentence—the meaning of which is debated to this day—however, what is not debated is the effect of that sentence. It snapped Phillips out of his depression and set him once again following God. After Lewis had spoken that cryptic sentence, he disappeared."

Now clean, Mr. Kindle slides his glasses back in place. "Phillips came out of his chambers only to find Lewis had died moments before the appearance, miles away. He pondered this in his heart with wonder, and never returned to his depression. Now, was this a case of God giving a soul a detour on the way to heaven for a special friend, to save him? Who knows? The fact that this encounter with a spirit was such a redemptive one leads me to believe it's an authentic encounter. However, only God knows for sure."

I'm confused by Mr. Kindle's sudden switch to being nice. However, over my many years, I've found adults can be quite unpredictable. Though I know in the company of other adults they are most likely saying the same thing about us. The difference is that with us, it's our insecurities and budding hormones making us do crazy things. For the adults, it is much more ego focused. They have such a rigid hold on what their reality should be, it becomes the catalyst pulling them off of the commonsense path. And my last encounter with a spittle spewing Mr. Kindle had him so far off that path that he couldn't possibly see it from where he was.

Mr. Kindle turns to leave, but I have one more question for him. "How would I know if the spirit is from God or from somewhere else?" I am genuinely curious about his answer.

Gathering himself for his big exit, he looks me in the eye. "Well, Miss Hill, I guess it would come down to the motivation. Is there a redemptive quality to the encounter? Will someone be helped or saved by the interaction? I can't imagine God bending his physical and moral laws for anything less." With that, Mr. Kindle turns with a flourish and departs for greener pastures.

Back in stalker mode and with a plan of action, I carefully approach

Stacia from behind, placing one foot in front of the other. Ten feet. Dropping my backpack, I switch my highlighter to my left hand. Seven feet. I remove the cap and slide the exposed point between my second and third fingers. Five feet. Stacia is on my left and I'm making a diagonal approach from behind her right shoulder. Three feet away now. Clueless, she hasn't yet caught on to my ninja-like stealthiness. One foot away, I can reach out and touch her. Stacia is wearing a t-shirt and I reach out grasping her arm just above the elbow.

"Hey, Stacia. What's going on?" I ask innocently. The highlighter is making contact while I keep my hand on Stacia's elbow.

"We just found out we have a scavenger hunt coming up. It's supposed to be a really big deal. We're going to be split into teams and have several hours to complete the hunt. It's supposed to help us get along and work together, but I have my doubts that'll happen, though." Stacia shakes her head, a wry smile on her face.

Removing my hand from her arm, I switch the highlighter to my right hand behind my back, keeping it out of Stacia's view. The marker has done its job and there is a nickel-sized green dot just above her elbow. "Sounds like fun. I haven't been on a scavenger hunt since Girl Scouts back in fourth grade."

"Knowing our camp staff, this is going to be a very different experience than a Girl Scout scavenger hunt," Kirsten says. "I'm guessing there'll be an element of danger involved. You know, alligator pits to cross, possibly automatic weapons fire to crawl underneath and certainly verbal abuse to keep us on our toes. A delightful experience for one and all."

"I just hope we live to tell about it," Stacia says.

"Me too," I reply. "The lawyers will need our testimony to put these guys where they belong." This gets a laugh. I get an elbow from Stacia as she jerks her head toward a nearby Mr. Johnson. His stern look is enough to get us moving toward the exit. I glance over my shoulder and find Mr. Johnson still watching us. We lock eyes for an instant. I can tell one thing for certain, there is no love in his gaze. Though he was close enough, I'm praying he hadn't heard our conversation. I do not want to get any further on Mr. Johnson's bad side, as I already have a very large target painted on my back.

Heading back to Grimm Hall after our gathering time, I spot a pale blue sweater up ahead, knowing this is my moment. Speeding up, I close up the gap. "Hey, Truly," I say touching her right shoulder. She turns smiling. I let a look of disgust cross my face as I jerk my arm away. "Oh gross."

"What?" she demands. "What is it?"

"There's a big spider on the back of your sleeve. Gross," I say.

Truly has a moment of panic and frantically pulls off the sweater, shaking it to dislodge the spider. The thing is, there wasn't a spider.

There is, however, a green dot just above her elbow. Gotcha.

18 | DON'T QUIT YOUR DAY JOB TO BECOME A MOTIVATIONAL SPEAKER

The morning comes way too early—and so does our physical training. Facing our über training instructor, Mr. Johnson is not the way I prefer to start my day. At least give me a latte to take a little of his edge off.

The room is buzzing with talk of the upcoming scavenger hunt. Speculation abounds. Mr. Johnson's entrance quiets the room as he holds up his hand looking for our full attention. He glances around the room, pausing at certain students. I am one of the lucky ones and his look speaks volumes as he stares at me. I am not and never will be one of his pets. I'm okay with that. I don't particularly care for him either.

"I want to take a moment to brief you on our upcoming scavenger hunt. This hunt will not be like others you might have had the pleasure of participating in. This will be a rigorous test of your mental and physical abilities. I will be assigning teams of four individuals to work together to complete your set of clues. If you do not function together, you will fail. If you do not use your brains, you will fail. And if you do not use your maximum physical abilities, you will fail."

He pauses, looking around the room. I lean over to Stacia. "He's a shining ray of sunshine, isn't he?" I whisper.

"If I were him, I wouldn't quit my day job to become a motivational speaker."

Just like sitting in church as a child, once I start to giggle, there is no stopping me. I try to hide it, but I'm unsuccessful and Mr. Johnson's gaze quickly slides my way. Facing certain punishment, I start coughing.

"I need water," I gasp out between coughs. Turning away, I head for the water fountain. I'm still giggling as I lean down to get a drink. With a supreme effort, I regain enough composure to rejoin the group. Getting a wary look from Mr. Johnson, he pauses for a long moment giving me the staredown. Me, I just offer my sweetest smile while I'm counting backward from 100 to keep my mind off of potential giggles. I get down to 84 before he gives up on me and returns to the other 20 kids in the room.

"The scavenger hunt will take place next Friday. It will take the top teams at least two hours to complete the hunt, while those teams with underachievers," he says and I swear he made a point to look at me, "will be lucky to finish in under four hours. Do you want to know what you're playing for?"

This is the part of Survivor where Jeff Probst—the host—tells the group what fabulous prize will be theirs when they outwit, outlast and outplay the other team. I like this part, and the group sounds excited as he makes them wait for the answer.

"Pride," he says, enjoying the disappointed groans around the room. This is the first moment I've seen him smile without looking like a hyena ready to bite the legs off of a wounded animal. "The pride that comes from doing a job well. What better reward could there possibly be?"

Not waiting for our answer, Mr. Johnson continues, "Let's get to the morning fun. We'll start with plyometrics and finish with some good old-fashioned rope climbing. I hope you are ready to sweat."

Trying to keep a positive attitude, I keep repeating, "What does not kill me, makes me stronger. What doesn't kill me..."

More fun than a girl should be allowed to have.

Back in my room, I'm paging through the book on Venezuela Ms. Neuman surprised me with. The book is recent, published just this year. I'm surprised by how different the various parts of the country can be. The larger cities appear to be modern while other parts of the country are virtually prehistoric. Reading about the life there, I pick up on the spirit of the people, the sort of spirit that would be attractive to my mother. There is exuberance for life there, allowing for a positive outlook despite less than ideal conditions. My mom was always a positive person and appreciated that quality in others.

Having Colombia as a neighbor apparently has its challenges. The Colombian drug cartel's influence has damaged Venezuela in many ways. Besides the spread of drugs, kidnapping has been rampant. The cartels hold people captive for ransom, asking for exorbitant sums of money—especially for such a poor country. It was an early theory that my mom was kidnapped, but no ransom was ever demanded. The book portrays the tragedy of how many of Venezuela's youth are corrupted by the lure of the cartel's money. They leave their families behind for a life of crime, violence and greed, forgetting the very values holding their family together in the first place.

Many of the Colombian drug processing facilities are located inside the insubstantial borders of Venezuela. Basically jungles, there isn't enough law enforcement to deter their criminal activities there. The cartels are free to do whatever they want in these compounds.

The chemicals used in the drug manufacturing process have hurt Venezuela's environment. Venezuela doesn't have the controls that the US has; there isn't an Environmental Protection Agency to monitor the process. Chemicals are dumped, infecting the ecosystem for miles around as well as much further downstream from the drug manufacturing facility. The effects can be quite devastating. The book details the recent account of a mass kill of amphibians traced to the spillage of chemicals used for drug processing. The actual spill had occurred miles upstream from where the kill had taken place.

"Hey," Stacia says as she jumps on my bed. "What are you doing?" She looks at the book cover in my hand. She gives me a little roll of her eyes, knowing the book came from my favorite counselor, Ms. Neuman.

"I thought I should at least look at it." I set the book down, looking at Stacia. "Maybe I am learning something here at camp. I'm realizing I can't duck and hide from who I am."

Crossing my legs, I lean forward. "Sure, there have been injustices, so what? Life isn't always fair. But I need to focus on my present and start preparing for my future. I feel that's why I am here. This camp—despite its numerous faults—has changed me. I am looking at things differently, realizing I need to understand who I am and be willing to take on whatever life throws at me. I am not the same naïve girl who first arrived here."

Stacia is nodding. "I like it. You're kicking butt and taking names."

"Whatever that means."

Stacia grins. "You went from princess to warrior."

"Exactly. I'm not avoiding the difficult situations, I'm meeting them head on. I remember a quote from the Art of War: If you know the enemy and know yourself, you need not fear the result of a hundred battles. From now on, that's how I roll."

I hold up the book. "After my mom's disappearance, I tried not to think about her. It was too painful. I did not want to hear about Venezuela or even South America. But that part of the world was important to my mother. And now, from reading about Venezuela, I can see the struggles they have to deal with every day. It certainly puts my camp experience into perspective."

"I don't know anything about South America. What kind of struggles are we talking about?" Stacia asks.

"I was reading about the area of Venezuela bordering Colombia. The drug cartels are destroying not only the environment but their entire way of life. They recruit young people and make them soldiers of the cartel, so it's nearly impossible to stop them. And the chemicals used in the drug processing are dumped directly into the water with no concern for the harm it causes downstream. There was this mass kill of amphibians…"

"Amphibians? You mean like frogs?"

"Yeah, there were thousands killed…" I look at Stacia. Her expression is enough to connect my obviously slow brain synapses. "Oh, my…."

Stacia grabs the book from me. Frantically paging through the book, she pauses and thrusts the book at me. I'm looking at a large picture of a marsh-like field. Photographed from a low angle, the picture shows a man kneeling by a metal pail. He's wearing mud-caked rubber boots, canvas shorts and a handkerchief pulled over his lower face—presumably to help him deal with the stench. The stench arising from all the dead frogs surrounding him. There have to be thousands in the picture. Little white bellies motionless in the mud as far as the camera's eye can see.

What does it mean? Could it really be a coincidence that the oddest thing that's ever happened to me—and that's saying a lot—also happened in the same country where my mother disappeared? "Do you believe in coincidences?" I ask Stacia. She's shaking her head, her eyes deer-in-the-headlights wide. "Me neither."

19 | FALLING COWS

I'm waiting outside Ms. Neuman's office, trying to overhear her conversation with Amanda. Amanda is this perfect looking girl from the suburbs. She seems nice enough except for the fact that she likes to start fires. At least that's the rumor about her. Of course, you can't believe everything you hear around this place. Just to be on the safe side, I'm not leaving any dry kindling lying around my room. A girl can't be too safe.

I hear muffled voices from behind the closed door, but nothing else. Frustrated, I get up and move closer—just as the door opens. Surprised by the door and not wanting to get caught, I quickly move back as Ms. Neuman opens the door, gesturing for Amanda to go first. Amanda may suspect I was eavesdropping as she is giving me the stink eye. Not wanting to sink to her level, I just stick out my tongue at her. I get the desired reaction, her mouth wide open.

"Come on in, Abbey," Ms. Neuman says, oblivious to Amanda's juvenile behavior.

I take my customary spot across from Ms. Neuman, tucking my legs underneath me. I look at Ms. Neuman, letting her speak first. After all, it's her agenda, not mine.

"Have you had an opportunity to look through the book I gave you?"

I nod.

"How did it make you feel? Since your mother loved the country so fondly, we're you able to see what captivated her about the people?"

I have already decided not going to mention my discovery. No good could come from raising those issues. "Well," I begin, "it was interesting to read about the people my mom cared for. I can see what led her to return to Venezuela time after time. She loved the spirit of the people there. Despite all the challenges they face, their positive attitude never quits."

Ms. Neuman nods. "I see. Let me ask you a question. After your mom disappeared and you realized she wouldn't be coming back, did you quit? Did you give up on being her daughter and having her as your mother? Did you push away your memories of her?" She tucks a stray strand of hair behind her ear and leans in close. "And didn't it leave a hole in your heart—one that just happens to be shaped in your mother's image?"

I'm crying now. I can't help it. "But it was so sudden. She was just ripped away from us, there was no warning..." There are no more words, only sobs.

Getting up from her chair, Ms. Neuman kneels in front of me. "Abbey, I am sorry. It is always that way. Things happen when you're not expecting them." She stands and removes a newspaper article pinned to her bulletin board. "I've kept this article as a reminder," she says, handing it to me.

The headline reads, *Falling cow crushes car*. Intrigued, I read on. *The Strunk family was on a family trip through the Oregon hills when the unlikely happened. A large cow fell from an overlooking cliff and totaled their car. A Chelan County fire chief says the family was lucky, missing being killed by a matter of inches. The 600-pound cow fell about 200 feet and landed on the hood of the Strunk's new Chrysler Pacifica. The fire chief believes the cow had fallen from a ledge overlooking the winding highway. No one was injured, however, the cow—and the Pacifica—were both beyond repair. 'I had no idea what had happened until it was over. We got out of the car, completely dazed, and found this very large cow lying across the hood of my new car,' Charles Strunk commented."*

I look up at Ms. Neuman, not getting the relevance. She said, "The thing is, Abbey, there will always be falling cows. Life isn't always going to be smooth and predictable. In your life, cows will drop. You won't see them coming, and you won't know what happened until it's over. The only thing you can do is accept it and roll with whatever life throws your way—or drops on you. Having the ability to cope and change directions at a moment's notice might just be the thing that keeps you alive."

Walking out the Wyman entrance, I couldn't help but stop and scan the skies. Falling cows. I can't say anyone has warned me about them before. This is such an odd place.

Boom. Boom. Boom. Boom. Boom. My heart racing, I lurch up in bed, startled out of my sleep by the heavy pounding on our door. I have no idea what time it is, but I know it's the middle of the night. Stacia is asleep on her bed across the room. How could she not have heard the pounding?

I can feel my heart hammering. The thing is, no one pounds on your door in the middle of the night with good news. I can't ignore the door, so I slide out of bed and creep over to it. My hand on the knob and I hesitate. Stacia is still asleep, her breathing slow and regular. Afraid the pounding will resume, I twist the deadbolt and slowly pull the door open.

This is the part I hate in scary movies. You know something is out there, and it is waiting for the victim—usually an unwitting teenage girl, much like myself—to step out. And they always do, leaving their position of safety to satisfy their curiosity. By all reports, it's been more than just cats that have suffered for their curiosity. People die too. Yet I step out from behind the door. It's never been me to ignore the unknown.

Empty. There is no one out here. Heavy pounding like I heard should have woken up everyone on this floor, yet mine is the only open door. Down the hall, I catch movement in the corner of my eye. The bathroom door is swinging shut. Closing the door behind me, I need answers and the best option for getting them just went into the bathroom. Barefoot, wearing only boxers and a t-shirt, I make my way down the hall.

At the bathroom door, I take a deep breath and push it open. The lights are off and my fingers scrape along the wall searching for the switch. Finding it, I flip the switch, firing up the ancient fluorescent lights mounted to the ceiling. Far from illuminating the room, the lights crackle and flicker, sporadically sending out harsh blue light followed by shadow. The effect is much like walking into a room lit by a single strobe light at the state fair haunted house.

The air is heavy with moisture, the mirrors fogged over. Given our early morning physical training, I can't imagine anyone up in the middle of the night taking a long shower—in the dark. Looking around the room as the light flickers on, it becomes clear that I am the only one here. I turn to leave and…

The line is drawn slowly, moving from top to bottom. It's as if a finger is touching the fogged mirror, drawing the symbol plaguing me for a week now. The unseen finger having finished the curved vertical line, starts adding the horizontal line, moving left to right. After a long moment, it is followed by a dot just off to the bottom right of the symbol. I can almost see the finger moving in a circle creating the dot. I'm frozen in place staring at the mysterious symbol, watching as condensation runs down the mirror.

The eerie flickering strobe effect of the light suddenly ends, the bathroom now bathed with cold blue light. I can't help shivering. Something catches my eye as I open the door, stopping me in my tracks. The symbol is now on each of the eight mirrors in the room.

20 | TROUBLE WITH TURNER

I am being pulled in way too many directions. I feel like the daycare teacher at snack time, with two-dozen sticky little hands pulling on you to get your attention. First, there's Turner, with his long dark hair covering those amazing eyes of his. Secondly, there's this camp I'm trying to survive with the mean staff and grueling physical challenges. And then there's this mysterious symbol that keeps showing up. I have this nagging feeling if I could get Turner off my mind for a while, I would be able to figure out the mystery behind the symbol.

After a tough morning of plyometrics—if I have to do jump squats ever again, it will be too soon—I found Turner. Soaked with sweat, his t-shirt clings to his ripped abs, demanding my attention. Turner's amused expression suggests he's noticed my attention. We walk down to the Kinnickinnic River and plop down by the riverbank. He leans back, fingers clasped behind his head and I do the same. It feels good to let the morning sun warm my tired body.

"Why are you here?" I ask, wanting to know what transgression landed Turner in this prison camp. So far, he has not shared anything about himself. A complete vault. Fairly typical for most boys. Better than the alternative—Tommy, for instance, whose favorite topic is Tommy.

Turner raises up onto an elbow. "Why am I here? Because you asked if

I wanted to go for a walk. You may have a good memory, however, it's a bit short." I get his grin.

"Funny. Tell me how you ended up spending your summer vacation here. Was it your idea?"

Shaking his head, Turner smiles. "Hardly. My father insisted. I wasn't exactly keen on the idea, as you might imagine. I have my doubts anyone would knowingly volunteer for this abuse." Turner lets out a big sigh. "My father—the former marine—said I lacked discipline. Discipline. How many 15-year-old kids do you know that are disciplined? Exactly. It's not like I was out stealing cars or robbing Quick-e-marts."

"Or rustling horses," I offer.

From the look on Turner's face, I've completely derailed his train of thought. "Or rustling horses…it was never bad things."

"What do you mean?" So there is a reason beyond strict parenting.

"I never tried to do anything mean or illegal."

"Turner, what did you do?"

"Nothing really." He looks guilty. If he'd been a cat, I wouldn't even have to look to know the canary was dinner. Turner won't look at me.

"Turner, spill. What did you do?" I let some exasperation creep into my voice.

"Just a few pranks is all."

I'm feeling some relief. This could have been so much worse. "Pranks?"

Turner nods.

"Like what? Give me an example." I fold my arms trying to look stubborn.

Looking down, he speaks softly, "I placed a fake ad on Craigslist claiming Robert Salisbury of Medina, Minnesota had abandoned his property and the Hennepin County Sheriff's Department was authorizing people to take away his belongings for free, including his horse. From what I gather, the only reason Salisbury came home to anything left in his house, was that a woman called him before she took his horse. She was worried about what to feed the horse. I guess Salisbury raced home to find at least 30 people rummaging through his house and his barn, loading his possessions into their cars and trucks and all of them refusing to give the stuff back. When he protested, claiming his stuff was not abandoned, people waved printouts of the Craigslist advertisement. They said this proved they were in the right to take his stuff. I thought it was hilarious they honestly believed just because it appeared on the internet, it was true. It boggles the mind."

OMG. I look at Turner absolutely astounded. "Are you nuts? You looked like a normal, high-functioning member of society. But no... Whatever made you think that was a good idea?"

Turner simply shrugs, so I press for more information. "Did you even know the guy, Salisbury?"

Still not holding my eyes, Turner says, "Salisbury was our school principal."

This made me fall right back into the grass. I couldn't help it, all I could do was laugh. It took a few long moments to regain my composure. Finally, I ask, "Why? What did he ever do to you?"

"Well, he did suspend me. Twice." There's that guilty look again.

"Umm... you don't get suspended for doing nothing." I sit up. "Turner, why were you suspended?"

"Which time?"

I roll my eyes at him. "Why don't you start with most recent time."

"I went into a deserted classroom and got into the ceiling. It was simple from there. I stripped the wiring from the speaker system, hooked up an amplifier and made my own school announcement. It was a beautiful spring day, after all."

"What was your announcement?"

Turner has a silly grin on his face. "I said due to a break in the water main, school was canceled for the rest of the day."

I look at Turner in a whole new light. "You are seriously deranged, you know that?"

He nods. He knows.

"I hate to ask, but what was your first suspension for?" Though I certainly do want to ask.

He has that grin again. "I just wanted to show some school spirit. What could be wrong with that? I went to East Middle School in Plymouth. Our big rival was West Middle School in Wayzata. Every year they always beat us in football. We play them twice each season and the first time they had killed us at home—the score was something like 37 - 3. Now we were going to play them in their Homecoming game. What better time to pull a little prank?" He looked at me for some encouragement or possibly validation. I just give him a casual nod, which is enough to keep him talking.

"It took a lot of planning, a lot of late nights, however when you're working toward a goal, it's no big deal."

I interrupt. "Have you tried using your powers for good, instead of evil?"

"Funny." Turner gazes at the clouds and continues. "I scouted out their stadium and made a grid of the main four sections directly across from the visitor's seats. I printed up a mess of signs in black and white, each one tied to a specific seat. The signs said the school boosters want to honor the coach and for everyone to hold up their signs at the beginning of the third quarter. What they didn't realize was, when held up together the signs actually spelled out, 'West Sucks.' I had warned some of my friends to have their video cameras ready to capture the event for YouTube. I probably went a bit too far notifying the scoreboard camera operator so he could film the coach's tribute. I believe it may have been my crowning achievement of middle school to see West Sucks up there on their fancy new scoreboard.

"My principal somehow learned I was behind the prank and called me to his office. Salisbury chewed me out for being mean-spirited and for showing unsportsmanlike behavior. Even as he was yelling at me, I thought I detected a twinkle in his eye, that maybe unofficially, he had enjoyed the prank. I got a three-day vacation for that one."

I had to smile. "That was pretty clever. How does one get started with pranks?"

"It began with telemarketers at first. They always called at the most inopportune times, at dinner or early Saturday mornings when I was trying to sleep. I decided to have some fun at their expense and started answering yes to every question, whether or not it was a yes or no question. They would eventually catch on and hang up on me.

Sometimes I would put on my best Middle Eastern accent and ask them totally inappropriate questions about their personal life. Other times, I would flirt shamelessly, hitting on whoever happened to be on the phone—it didn't make a difference if it was male or female. The more awkward, the better. I lived to torment those people."

I'm laughing. "I will be staying on your good side. You can be quite dangerous." As I'm holding his eyes, the mood changes. I can feel the shift, as we both grow quiet, my pulse quickening, his dark eyes looking right into my soul. Turner leans into my space.

"Hey, let's go," a voice calls out to ruin the moment. "Camp meeting."

Really? It would have been perfect, so perfect.

21 | MAYBE THEY FOUND OUT ABOUT THE TOILET THING

I'm standing in front of a firing squad. I feel my knees tremble. My heart is pounding in my chest as they stare at me. I hope they will just hurry and get it over with.

We are gathered at the fire pit area, maybe 20 of us troubled teens and the dozen or so camp staff. They stand across from us, maybe not a firing squad, but it feels very "us versus them." I'm not the only nervous one here as we wait for the meeting to begin. There is plenty of whispering as everyone speculates about the reason for the meeting.

"Maybe the scavenger hunt is canceled."

"I bet they want to apologize for being so mean to us."

"Maybe they found out about the toilet thing."

"What if they want us to stay longer? I can't miss school."

"Suppose they got word the mothership was coming back for the counselors?"

"I swear I only took one. Okay, maybe it was two. But no more than four."

"We're being forced to join the glee club. I knew this place sucked."

"When's lunch?"

"It's the ghost thing." I swear the girl glanced in my direction as she said this. I look away.

The same dour faced man who wouldn't help me escape from this camp holds up his hand. The whispering quiets quickly. His face has no expression whatsoever. This is a man who wouldn't smile even when the lottery official was handing him the oversize check in front of the cameras during the obligatory press conference. This man has no joy in his heart—clearly he wasn't a breastfed baby, as my father would say.

"Our annual scavenger hunt starts today right after dinner. I have broken you out into teams of four. And no, there will be no switching players between teams. We have eight teams competing." He pauses, looking around the group. He gives a slight nod toward the camp staff. "We have decided to offer a little incentive this year. The top four teams will be allowed to miss physical training next week. However, the bottom four will be doing two-a-day physical training sessions all week long." There is a unison groan echoing my sentiment at the prospect of seeing Mr. Johnson two times each day—for a week straight.

"Trust me, you do not want to be in the bottom four. The workouts will be particularly...difficult." Oddly enough, there was almost a hint of a smile there. Figures.

The staff spread out, each with a sheet of paper in hand. Mr. Johnson speaks first, "When you hear your name, come join your teammates and strategize a bit. You have to work together as a team to achieve your goal. However, you will not be able to see your first clue until the start of the competition tonight." He nods to one of the staff members.

A counselor holds up his sheet of paper and begins to read. "Corey

Palmer, Kirsten Anderson, Salina Prescott and Makao Day." The four tentatively move towards the counselor, unsure what to do next.

Mr. Johnson is next in line. He reads his four names, butchering the pronunciation of three out of the four names. I suspect he was doing it intentionally, as most people would have little difficulty with "Smith." He pronounces it as "Smitts."

My name still has not been read as Charlotte reads her list. I glance over at Stacia and she just shrugs.

Mr. Kindle slowly reads the names off his list, over-enunciating each name. Mine was not one of them.

An older counselor I've never met reads from her list. She puts on her reading glasses after pushing the list away as far as her arms would reach. There is a snicker off to my left. My name is not on her list either. Three more teams to go.

The next two counselors in read their list of names. I keep waiting to hear my name as the crowd shrinks to a handful. I glance around seeing Carrie is also waiting. I close my eyes and repeat in my head, "Please, not Carrie, anyone else, but not Carrie."

When the counselors are finished, it is only Ms. Neuman left holding her list. I glance around seeing Carrie is still waiting. Wonderful. Next to me is Stacia, thankfully. That makes three so far. Who is the final person on our team? Looking behind me, I see it's Turner. He gives me a wry smile. Once again, we are thrown together.

Ms. Neuman glances around. "No need to read my list. Come on up, guys."

There are times in life when you start seeing patterns emerge. Circumstances don't seem so circumstantial when they are repeated time and time again. The same people seem to turn up again and again. Can it really be a coincidence? Maybe we are just part of a larger plan and for good or bad, certain people are placed in our path. If this is true, I wish the plan had been shared with me first. Is it too much to ask for a little control of my own life?

I look over at Carrie. She looks at me. No emotion crosses her impassive face. As a realist, I may not like Carrie, but her athletic ability can only help our team. Stacia is on the other end of the scale: not tall, slight build, no real muscle to speak of. She is whip-smart, though. If there's a puzzle to be figured out, she's the one I want on my side. Turner is an excellent addition as well. I realize my judgment may be a bit swayed where Turner's concerned, but his strength can only help us. As he charges through the obstacles, I will be right behind him.

"What's to strategize?" Stacia asks. "We won't know anything until we get the clues. Let's split up, we could get through the list in half the time."

Ms. Neuman is shaking her head. "You're missing the point. We want you to work together. This exercise forces the players to work together for a common goal. So put it this way, splitting up will disqualify you and guarantee you a spot in the bottom four." She looks at each of us, holding our eyes for a long moment, the challenge evident in her dark eyes. "Anyone want to volunteer for two-a-day physical training workouts?"

None of us say a word. Clearly, we don't have to.

"Good luck tonight," Ms. Neuman says with a long pause before she turns and walks away. I have the distinct feeling she wanted to add, "You'll need it." Whatever. Me and my "A game" will be ready.

22 | ALL THE WORLD'S A STAGE

My heart is pounding as we race toward our first destination in the scavenger hunt. This whole thing feels like it's out of control. First, they changed the rules on us. Every scavenger hunt I had ever been on, we were given our list of items to gather. Sure, it was at Brittany's 8th birthday party, but my partner Eva and I were the winners. We totally crushed the other girls. Ahh, good times.

For this scavenger hunt, each team was handed a rolled up scroll of paper and instead of a list, we found a single clue. Each clue we solve leads us to the next one. Apparently, we are required to use our mental abilities as well as our physical prowess—though the first clue was totally obvious.

> *As a matter of course*
> *Just remember that before you slide*
> *This place can be a climb for some,*
> *But not an obstacle for others.*

This clue could be referring to only one place. You have to climb the wall to get up to the platform—just before you slide down. When Turner read the clue out loud, we all shout in unison, "the obstacle course."

The second thing leaving me feeling out of control is Carrie, who is not exactly the ideal team player. After reading the clue, she immediately sprints for the course, leaving us behind. After a moment's hesitation, Turner takes off after her. Stacia and I look at each other, shrug and sprint after them as we try to catch up. Way to be a team.

I can feel the sweat soaking through my t-shirt as I make my way up the hill, pulling Stacia along with me. The summer heat has lasted well into the evening. The air is thick and muggy, with the temperature hovering around 90 degrees. This time of year, the heat and moisture charge the atmosphere with enough energy to bring in some spectacular thunderstorms and even the occasional tornado. The sky is a bit hazy, but I don't see any threatening clouds on the horizon—which is good considering my fear of storms.

Carrie arrives at the obstacle course and dives for the tunnel after making quick work of the tires. Me, I'm too busy laughing. "Guys, we're not running the obstacle course, we're just picking up the clue."

All three of us are standing by the tunnel's exit as Carrie pokes her head out. "Having fun?" Turner asks her, a smile on his face. "Let's focus on the job, you can always come back and finish the course on your own time." Carrie obviously does not like being teased, as she communicates her rebuttal with a single finger.

Stacia is already three-quarters the way up to the platform when we turn around. "So, we'll just wait down here, then?" I call up to her.

"Uh, huh." And she climbs onto the platform, moving out of sight.

It doesn't take her long as there's a loud whoop and Stacia launches herself down the slide. She ends up sprawled out in the sand at the bottom, the scroll held tightly in her raised fist. "Yeah, baby," she says, the joy evident in her voice.

I pluck the scroll from her hand and slide off the light blue ribbon. The others crowd around to read the clue.

The Kinnickinnic River is fun to say,
As well as a great place to stay.
If I gave up poetry to be an actor,
This is where I would like to play.

"The river." Turner points toward the nearby river. Carrie grabs his hand and redirects it.

"Not so fast," she says. "They mean the Kinnickinnic River Theater."

"Carrie's right." I can't believe those words came out of my mouth. "The clue also mentions being an actor."

Stacia joins in. "And being in a play."

"Of course," Turner says. "Though I want to go on record right now, the clue writer should give up the poetry gig. For me, a poem that isn't classically structured is a complete waste of our time. The verses fall short of conveying the powerful imagery and emotion that can be truly transformational."

We all just stop and look at Turner. Stacia has her mouth hanging open, while Carrie is giving Turner the lovesick puppy look most teenage girls reserve for the picture of Justin Bieber cut out of Seventeen magazine and taped to their bathroom mirror. Gag me with a spoon.

"Hold on," I say, smelling something fishy here. "Turner, I had no idea you were such an expert in literature. What exactly do you mean when you say a poem is classically structured?"

Turner has the look of sheepish embarrassment I see when I catch my father with a gas problem. "You know," he offers.

I'm not letting him off the hook here. "Pretend I know nothing about poetry. Pretend I'm not familiar with rhyming patterns, meter, grammar and imagery. I know nothing of how linguistic and intentional structures function in counterpoint to the metrical and stanzaic structures to create something far greater than the sum of its words. C'mon, humor me, Turner."

Shaking his head, Turner mumbles something incoherent.

"Pardon me?" I ask.

Turner looks me in the eye, regaining some of his usual swagger. "You can't trust any poem that doesn't begin with 'Roses are red; violets are blue.' I'm right, aren't I?"

I burst out laughing. The other two quickly join me. "You are such an idiot," I say shaking my head.

"Maybe. But you have to admit I'm the nicest retard you know."

This time, it's easy to admit: he is right.

The University Center is deserted tonight. Everyone must be involved in the scavenger hunt and as if to prove my theory, another group races by, no doubt chasing down a clue. I hear a whoop of laughter as they round the corner at the end of the street. We pause as a crackle of thunder ripples across the summer sky. I shudder, here it comes.

Once inside, we take the stairs two at a time and reach the Kinnickinnic River Theater in a few moments. Outside, the air was so thick with humidity, I was sweating like crazy. In here, the air conditioning is cranked up so high, I'm shivering. Somewhere in the middle of those two extremes would be nice.

Stacia is looking at me, and it takes a moment before I catch on to her unspoken fear. Confidently, I grab a hold of her hand and whisper that it'll be fine, no more moving seats. Carrie and Turner follow us into the dimly lit theater.

A single overhead spotlight illuminates a circular portion of the stage no larger than a hula hoop. Clearly this is the spot. We take the stage as a group, as Stacia and I warily glance around. Fortunately, not even a single chair is acting out of line. At the lighted circle—expecting to find another rolled up scroll in the center of the circle—I'm perplexed when it isn't there.

"Okay," Turner voices our concern, "where's our clue?" He turns in place looking around.

"It has to be here somewhere," Carrie says. "Let's spread out." Carrie heads to stage right, and Stacia shrugs, turning toward the other end of the stage. I head for the darkness of the backstage area looking for a clue, feeling oddly like one of the girls in a Scooby Doo episode. Oh well, time to get jinky with it.

The overhead spot gives me just enough light to make out indistinct shapes floating into my field of vision as I move further into the dark. Hopefully, I'll be able to avoid running into sharp objects as I slowly make my way further into the gloom. Just to be safe, I shuffle along slowly with my arms outstretched looking like some bad movie zombie. Soon, a distant glow catches my attention. The neon green light is so diffused; it looks as if I'm seeing it through a dense fog. As I get closer, the shape begins to coalesce.

I can feel the hair on the back of my neck stand up one by one as my brain makes sense of what's in front of me. It's the symbol again. The day glow paint looks like it was freshly painted—as I watch the green paint run down the rough brick wall. I'm fairly sure this paint is not available at my local Home Depot. I stare at the mark for a long minute, feeling helpless. I have no idea what it means.

I hear Turner, maybe 20 yards behind me. He's speaking in a loud, over-the-top theatrical style voice.

> *"All the world's a stage, and all the men*
> *and women merely players: they have*
> *their exits and their entrances; and one*
> *man in his time plays many parts,*
> *his acts being seven ages."*

I make my way onto the stage just as Turner is finishing, thrusting his hand up in dramatic fashion, still standing in the lighted circle. I break out into spontaneous applause as I hear Stacia give a loud whistle, her fingers in the corners of her mouth. With a loud click, an overhead projector is brought to life. Rather than facing the stage for the audience to see, the projected screen has lit up the back wall, clearly meant for the stage actors view only. And just like that, we have our next clue.

> *Some may ask, "Why boy?"*
> *However in a decade's time,*
> *The question will change,*
> *The answer just simple steps before you enter.*

23 | FLASHES OF LIGHTNING, ROLLS OF THUNDER

"You just needed to be an actor on stage, reciting lines from that Rodgers and Hammerstein musical," Stacia says as we gather around looking up at the words projected on the back wall. "There must be someone here, someplace." She looks around.

"Umm, that was actually Shakespeare," Turner says uncomfortably.

"I didn't know he wrote musicals," Stacia responds with a twinkle in her eye. "What do you suppose our clue means?" she asks, looking back up at the enigmatic verses.

"Why boy?" Carrie says this out loud as she shifts her weight from side to side. "Why boy?"

"Why ask why?" Turner says to nobody in particular.

The projector picks this moment to go black, the words fading into the wall.

After a moment's hesitation, we make our way up the aisle, anxious to get out of the theater. "Why boy?" Carrie says again.

"How would the question change after a decade?" Stacia asks.

"Good question," I offer.

"Thank you," she replies. "A decade is ten years. What happens after ten years to a boy?"

We all look to Turner as we make our way down the steps into the University Center lobby. Another group is leaving out the front entrance. "Well?" Carrie asks Turner.

He holds up his palms, shrugging. "He gets taller, stronger. His voice gets lower. He starts growing hair in funny places."

I elbow Turner. "Most of that happens to a girl as well, you know. Maybe not the voice thing." We step out into the humid air as a nearby rumble of thunder suggests threatening weather is fast approaching. "Our clue writer clearly makes the distinction it's a boy we are discussing. What else happens to a boy after ten years?"

Turner hesitates. "I don't know...he just becomes a man, I guess." Smiling, he flexes his bicep. I like it.

"Why boy?" Carrie repeats. "Why man? Why man?"

"The Wyman Education Building!" I yell, unable to keep cool. "It has to mean the Wyman building."

"That has to be it," Stacia agrees. "What else did the clue say?"

"Just simple steps..."

"...before you can enter."

Obvious. We head down the sidewalk at a run, feeling the urgency as a flash of lightning crackles overhead. The Wyman building is directly across a large grass courtyard from the University Center. However, after our experience with the squishy dead frogs, we stick to the sidewalk.

Within a few minutes, we are at the steps. Sticking out of the wrought iron handrail is another rolled up scroll. It's in my hands before the others can grab it. I slide the blue ribbon off and uncurl the stiff parchment.

It's not a darker hall,

nor a hall filled with spiders,

yet for Peter, it will echo,

"Two, two, two."

This time, it's not so obvious. We huddle, another flash of lightning crackling overhead. Another shudder.

"This one is tough," I offer.

"I don't get it." Carrie frowns.

"Me neither," Stacia adds. Stacia is the one I was counting on for these puzzles. She tries to redeem herself, though. "Let's break it down. Not a darker hall. A light hall then?"

"There are a lot of halls here. The buildings are full of them." Carrie is clearly a master of the obvious.

"You know," Stacia says, "A lot of the buildings are named, 'Something Hall.' Maybe the clue is pointing to a particular hall."

"Peter Hall?" Carrie again.

"There's not a Peter Hall," Turner says and starts laughing.

"What?" I demand.

"I know where the clue is, c'mon." Heading back in the direction we had just come from, running in a tight group, we look to Turner for an explanation. He keeps us waiting. "This way," is all we get as we continue on Wild Rose Avenue past the University Center.

Flashes of lightning, rolls of thunder. The sky comes alive as the last of our daylight creeps out of sight. I glance at my nonexistent watch. It's not that late, is it? It should be light for another hour this time of year. A fleeting glimpse tells me it's the mass of dark storm clouds centered over the campus that is responsible for keeping the light away. An omen? I don't believe in omens. However, it couldn't hurt to exercise some caution. You never know when a cow may be dropping your way.

We make our way past the deserted Rodli Hall building, another of the campus buildings under construction. Dark shapes inside the windows manifest themselves as threatening figures to my hyper imagination. I clearly have been under too much stress for way too long. The physical and mental challenges have been taking their toll on me. Next summer, no camp for me—it's Disney or nothing.

We pass our home, Grimm Hall. It doesn't feel like home, but it's the closest thing I've got here. Any place I can consistently lay my head down works for me. Parker Hall is the next building we come to and Turner steers us toward the entrance. "Parker Hall?" I ask.

"Yeah, Parker Hall," he replies. "You may not realize it, but I'm a closet geek."

"Oh, we realize it," Stacia says with a smile. She's always ready to dish it out.

Turner ignores her. "I've collected comic books since I first learned to read. Spiderman has always been my favorite. I could identify with the nerdy teenager," he pauses, looking at Stacia. "Nothing out of you."

Stacia simply holds up her hands, palms out.

"That nerdy teenager was bitten by a radioactive spider. His name was Peter Parker." He pauses, waiting for us to catch on. We look at each other blankly.

"You don't get it? The clue mentions a darker hall, which rhymes with Parker Hall. It also mentions Peter and spiders. Obvious, right?"

"Obvious—if you're a geek. Hey, you said it first," Stacia says holding up her hands.

"What are we waiting for? Let's go." I say, moving toward the entrance.

"Where to?" Carrie asks, still standing in place.

"Room 222," I say. "The final part of the clue."

Upstairs, we slowly open the door—the numbers 222 stenciled on the old wooden door—as the door creaks open in protest. There is a creepy feeling about the place, and it's not just me. No one wants to be the first to enter. But the thing is, we need the clue, so I warily step into the room.

The room is completely deserted, not a single piece of furniture on the floor, not a single picture hanging on the wall. Gray carpeting, gray walls. Seriously, this place needs to be on Pimp my Dorm Room. Where are the reality TV people when you need them? The sparseness does have one benefit though: it's obvious the clue isn't here.

"Nothing here," I say to my three teammates waiting at the door. They decide to join me and push into the room. We're all back to back, facing different directions looking for the clue. I don't see it.

"Are you sure," Carrie starts, as she levels a condescending look at Turner, "we are in the right place? Maybe you should have spent more time reading real books."

I look to Turner, who has that incredulous "you're throwing me under the bus after all I've done" look. His eyes are burning a hole in Carrie and I can almost see the anger rising in him. "A real book? Like what, Twilight? The Sisterhood of the Traveling Pants? Please."

Carrie takes a step closer toward Turner. "I read only non-fiction. Why give up the opportunity to learn real things from real people? Besides," she pauses, "everyone knows that Wonder Woman could take Spiderman in a fair fight."

We all shift our gaze, waiting for Turner's response. He doesn't keep us waiting. "You know, the last time I saw a woman in boots, wearing short shorts and carrying a magic lasso, she was being arrested in downtown Minneapolis for prostitution." Turner steps into Carrie's space, puffing out his chest. For the life of me, I can't tell if he's angry or having fun at Carrie's expense. Either way, I'm good with it. "And you honestly can't see a benefit from reading a book that sprung from someone's imagination? To boldly go where no one has gone before? Even Einstein said logic can take you from point A to point B, while imagination can take you anywhere."

Wanting to get us back on track, I hook my arm in his and pull him toward the door. "Come on, Captain Kirk. We need to rise above this argument." I pause, glancing above the door. It's there, hidden in a decorative tangle of vines, dried berries and stems. A rolled up scroll of paper tied with a baby blue ribbon. "The wall hanging…" I say.

Turner reaches for it, plucking our next clue from its hiding place. I can't wait to see where this one will take us.

24 | FAR FROM THE EDGE

If your fear is one of heights,
Or burns on your hands,
You may never reach the clue you seek.
There is one hope for you, and his name is Jim.

Things are looking up. An easy clue for a change. "Gonna be climbing some rope in the gym," I say. "My favorite."

"Mine too," Stacia says with a grin. "I enjoy having my shoulders pulled from their sockets." Stacia steps out into the hallway after waving Carrie to go first. "On the plus side, we are getting closer to being done with this scavenger hunt."

"Good thing, the weather is starting to look dangerous out there." The door is mostly glass and the lightning outside is near constant, one bright flash being overlapped by the next, looking every bit a paparazzi-stalked Taylor Swift appearance. I've never liked storms. Ever since I was a little girl, storms have terrified me. If there were even a slight chance of severe weather, I would be paralyzed by my fear of what might happen—I wouldn't go anywhere or see any of my friends. And whenever a storm threatened, I would be glued to the weather channel, too afraid to do anything else. My fear got so bad that the first thing I would do each morning was look at the day's forecast and check the weather radar. Learning about the weather is probably what made this fear diminish and go away over time. The plus side of living in fear all those years is I became almost television meteorologist adept at reading the signs. I could always tell if things were going to blow over or blow up in our faces. We push through the door and I know instantly this storm isn't blowing over.

The sky is a sickly green color, the rotation of the clouds overhead obvious as my old fears suddenly awaken. My feet stop moving, their link to my brain severed by my near panic. My breathing has sped up and even though I try to regain some semblance of control, I can hear myself panting.

"Abbey."

I want to run. I can't move, though.

"Abbey!"

Someone is saying something. I feel far removed from the others in the group. My vision has closed up, all peripheral vision gone. I know I need to move, get out of this storm. Even when I feel the hail begin to strike, I am held in place.

"Abbey. Are you with me?" My eyes slowly focus on Turner's. His hands are on my face, his eyes inches away from mine. "Time for us to leave," he says with an unusual combination of calm and urgency.

He grabs my hand, pulling me from my spot. Rather than get dragged by Turner, I gain strength from his touch and my feet regain their ability to move. My focus is on one thing: the door ahead. We race across the courtyard, feeling the sting of the marble-sized hail. I've never experienced anything like this, the closest being the paintballs I was on the receiving end of at a church youth group outing last summer. I'm definitely going to have welts again.

The door is just out of my reach as my hand stretches out. Time slows as I look at the door. Like most doors in older buildings, the door is a massive thing, made from oak, with rusted metal fittings. The surrounding wall is made of weathered river rock, cemented in place by craftsman a century before. It's the pattern in the oak beams that catch my eye. The wood grain is long and fluid, almost like liquid as it bends and flows like a river. In the darkest part of the grain, there is a similarity to the symbol I have seen relentlessly around the school here. The artful curve, the way it bends, the fluidity, something…

The moment is gone as the door opens in front of me and I find Stacia and Carrie waiting inside for us. I am less than gently urged forward by Turner's nudge in the center of my back. "Nice evening for a stroll, don't you think?" I ask to no one in particular.

"That hail is going to leave a mark," Turner says as he pulls off his t-shirt. The rest of us just sort of stop what we were doing—thinking, moving, breathing, like that—while a now shirtless Turner wrings out his soaked shirt, twisting it in his hands. The corded muscles stand out in his arms while his six-pack tenses with his effort. Good lord, I don't think I have ever seen someone so lean. The shirt is soon pulled back over his head and Turner looks around at our faces. "What?" he asks, clearly not getting it.

Carrie clears her throat, pulling us back to the reality of our lives. "The clue…" She lets her words hang there.

I try my best to string together some coherent thoughts. However, "The gym. The rope. Climbing," is the best I can do. In my defense, there are considerable changes that happen to a 14-year-old girl. Take hormones for example. I would be the first to admit the link between our brain and our bodies haven't been solid to begin with. But throw some hormones into the mix and look out. These days, our bodies have become fiercely independent and are likely to betray us at the drop of a …shirt.

The gym is mostly dark; the only light left burning is the center spotlight. Our goal is clearly lit: I can see our scroll hanging a foot or so from the ceiling—though it looks like a mile straight up. Four ropes hang in a circle surrounding it. There are two shorter lengths of cord lying on the ground below.

"I got this one," Turner says and begins to climb the rope with ease. The higher he gets, though, the easier it is to see he's too far from the scroll to reach it. Turner figures out the same thing and pauses five feet from the gym's ceiling.

"Try swinging," Carrie calls up to him.

"Good idea," he replies, shifting his weight to start his swinging motion. Turner is at full reach but is still a good five feet away from the scroll. The issue is, when you are so close to the ceiling, you don't have enough rope to move very much. He tries dropping another five feet and swinging again. This time, he gets more movement, but now he's too far below the scroll to get close.

"Try this," Carrie calls and tosses up one of the lengths of cord we found on the floor. Turner gives a valiant effort using the cord as a whip to knock the scroll loose. He's still not able to get close enough to knock it down. And after a few tries, he slides down.

"My arms are on fire," he says, shaking them. "I can't hold on and swing the rope well enough to knock the scroll loose. It looks to be secured pretty well." Turner's gaze lowers. I didn't expect this—Turner looks embarrassed by his failure on the ropes.

"Better than we could have done," I say trying to give him some pride back. "But now what?"

"I have an idea," Carrie says, picking up a section of rope. "Stacia, hang on to the other end while we climb." She points Stacia to the hanging rope diagonal from hers.

Carrie holds the end of her cord and uses it to pull herself closer to Stacia. I see what she's trying to do. "Hold on," I say. There has to be a reason for the second length of cord and the two other hanging ropes. "Let's loop this around the other the cord like this." It's sort of like making a + sign. My cord starts at the bottom at 6:00 and crosses theirs making a right angle turn ending at 3:00. Stacia gets it and switches to the 9:00 position with Carrie in the 12:00 spot. Turner holds the other end of our cord.

"Brilliant," he says. "This way we're pulling ourselves into the middle to release the scroll. They said we would have to work together. Teamwork, what a concept."

Turner stops talking as he realizes we are all staring at him. "I'm babbling, aren't I? My bad."

Making my way up the ropes, I'm clenching the end of my cord in my teeth—it's just too difficult to hold it and climb at the same time. At the top, we pull on our respective ends, tightening our group and bringing us close to the scroll. Turner has the longest reach and is soon able to untie the scroll from its rope. He holds it out for us to see and then drops it to the floor below. "Last one down is a loser," he says as he starts back down.

Carrie is the first to the floor after dropping the last six feet. Turner and Stacia are right behind. I am the last by a country mile, but I don't care. My hands are raw, my biceps burn, and my shoulders are threatening to detach themselves from their sockets. I'm just thankful to be on the ground again. Carrie holds up her thumb and index finger to her forehead giving me the near-universal "loser" sign. Not one to be outdone, I hold up a single finger, giving her the universal "I hope you have a long and happy life" sign. Or something like that.

Carrie slides the blue ribbon off the rolled up paper. The light from the spotlight illuminates the words.

> *If this place were smaller, a college it would be.*
> *Seeing it's not, my best advice would be*
> *To stay as far as possible from the edge.*
> *Searching for clues here can bring you up or bring you down.*

"What's larger than a college? A university," Stacia says as she answers her own question, her smile wide and her eyes twinkling. Stacia may have her theatrical moments as she explores her Truly self, but she wants to be accepted as much as the rest of us.

"You know, you're much smarter than your know-it-all sister. And better looking too." I tell Stacia, giving her a wink.

"Where has Truly been?" Carrie asks. "I don't recall seeing her when they gave out our team assignments." Carrie doesn't get it. I do.

"I think we have seen the last of her pale blue sweater," I say giving Stacia a grin. "Truly has been retired from public viewing. Elvis has left the camp." The astonished look on her face is priceless. In response to her questioning look, I just smile and nod. Yes, I know your little secret.

"Stay away from the edge as far as possible," Carrie paraphrases our clue. "What's far from the edge?"

"The middle?" I offer hesitantly.

"Ahh. So what's in the middle of the University?" Turner asks. "We need a map, because knowing our clue writer, we'll need to find the geographic center of the entire campus."

Stacia holds up her hand. Always one for the drama, she leaves it there waiting for our full attention. "Turner mentioned the geographic center. The center is also far from the edge. And get this: the University Center." I honestly think she wants to take a bow.

We all seem to get it at the same moment: the clue is directing us back to the University Center. And we're off running for the door, anxious to get the next clue.

That is, until I get to the door. I so don't want to go back out there in the storm. Turner steps up again to be my savior. "Do you trust me?"

I nod.

"Then all you have to do is hold my hand."

I can do that. In fact, I like doing that. A lot.

"Soon as we step outside, we run like the wind. That's it. You don't worry, you don't stop, you just think about getting to the University Center and figuring out the rest of our clue. It was something about bringing us up or down. Focus on that, okay?" His eyes hold mine, my fingers intertwined with his. Yes, I will follow this boy wherever he leads. Who cares about a little bit of bad weather?

25 | THE NUTCRACKER SUITE

I don't remember much about the weather. The hail had stopped, but the gusts of wind made me feel like I was a kite, fighting a losing battle to stay in one place. I simply held onto Turner's hand, allowing him to lead me through our weather apocalypse while I let my thoughts run free. The answer had come to me before we reached the end of the sidewalk. There was only one clear answer to the clue. What would be in the University Center that could bring you up or bring you down? See? It is obvious. The elevator.

It's good to be brilliant. However, I do find it tough to remain humble.

As we made our way through the storm to the University Center, I remember seeing the distant silhouette of a group running in the opposite direction. I can't be certain because the lightning flash gave only the most fleeting of a glimpse, but there looked to be five of them. Why five? That number stuck with me as we made it to the welcome sanctuary of the University Center. I point a finger toward the elevator, watching a drop of rainwater fall from the tip. "The clue is in the elevator."

Turner stabs a finger at the call button. The button lights up informing us the elevator has been summoned. Carrie arrives next and the first thing she does is push the already lit button. It might be human nature for each of us to have to push the elevator call button. I'm sure I've done the same thing at some point in my life. Though, because this is Carrie, it bugs me.

"So, you didn't think Turner pushed the elevator button correctly?" I ask, letting some of my irritation creep into my normally pleasant voice.

"Well, duh," she answers without hesitation. "If he had, the elevator would already be here, wouldn't it?" Carrie can give as good as she gets.

Leave it to Stacia to take things further. She steps over to the elevator panel and gives it a series of quick jabs. "You clearly do not have the touch either." At that precise moment, the elevator chime sounds announcing its arrival.

We look at each other and break out laughing. Maybe it's the near-constant tension, maybe it's the weather or maybe it's our pent up frustration with each other, but we all break out laughing. It's the kind of near hysterical laughter where you lose control of your body and find it's impossible to stay standing. ROFL is how I would text it.

The elevator opens while we are laughing and no one can make it inside before the door closes again. The elevator motor starts and the indicator light above shows it has moved on to the second floor. I'm thinking it's a good thing the door closed—although I don't believe the others saw what was on the elevator. A stern looking older man was pointing a finger directly at me. He was trying to convey something, but his meaning wasn't clear. Possibly a warning, the only thing clear was that it wasn't a good thing.

"Why did it leave?" Stacia asks. "Is there someone up there who pushed the button? What if they took our clue?"

Carrie's at the elevator call button in a flash. The hum of the motor starts immediately. I can feel the tension eating at us as the elevator descends. Turner pushes his way to the front, wanting to be there first when the doors open. Personally, I am okay with that. I don't need that angry man jabbing his finger at me again. While it hasn't exactly been unusual having dead people around me, there's something different going on here. Something with a greater sense of urgency.

The door opens. I hold my breath. Turner has his arms up like he's ready to pounce and tackle whoever's after our clue. But the elevator is empty—not even a finger-waving, stern-looking older man. We crowd into the elevator car, looking up, looking down, yet not finding the scroll. "Damn," Turner spits out.

"Did you actually expect it to be sitting out in the open?" Stacia says. "Things haven't been exactly obvious so far. Maybe in here," she says, opening the elevator's emergency phone box. The scroll is not obvious once again and Stacia lifts up the phone looking behind it. The scroll is not in the phone box.

Turner has his eyes fixed on the ceiling of the elevator. He starts jumping and pushing at the ceiling tile with his fingertips. His first touch raises the tile before it settles back into position again. His second jump leaves the tile askew, white fiber sprinkling down on us like a December snowfall. His third jump dislodges the tile sending it to the floor, now in three pieces. No scroll. Now what?

"Hello?"

All of us spin around to see Stacia with the elevator phone to her ear. She repeats the single word. "Hello?" Stacia's brow furls as she holds up her hand requesting our silence.

Stacia's voice has a monotone quality as she repeats aloud the words she is hearing. "Time is your friend as you search for this clue," she pauses, wanting us to remember our verbal clue. Stacia continues, "though getting fired at camp would bring you up to nine, not ten."

A long pause.

"That's it. They hung up." Stacia returns the phone to the box.

"How did the clue begin?" I ask.

"Time is your friend—our friend, I guess." Carrie pauses, clearly having a thought on the clue. We pause as well and wait for her to continue. "I think it must be related to a clock," she says.

"Sounds like that might be it," I offer as we step off the elevator. "There's a clock outside the gym. The one that chimes at random times."

"It does?"

"I've never heard it do that."

"Me neither."

Whatever. Apparently the clock chimed just for me on my first day here. Okay, I know what you're thinking, what's one more strange thing in a very strange life? But why? Why does it always have to happen to me?

"Hey," Turner says, bouncing in his spot. "It also said getting fired at camp would bring you up to nine, not ten. It must mean the nine o'clock position. The clue is at the nine." He smiles. "Let's go."

The group is moving toward the entrance, eager to find the clue.

"Excuse me," I call, still standing outside the elevator. "I don't want to rain on our parade, but what's the deal with getting fired at camp? That doesn't fit with the clock thing." The other three look at me, slightly crestfallen. Actually, they are looking at me like I am the older sister at the birthday party letting air out of the kid's balloons. I know, I am such the fun sucker.

"Fired at camp?" Carrie spits. "How could we get fired at camp?"

"I know," I offer. "They won't let us leave. I even hired a lawyer, but no luck."

Ignoring me, Carrie is thinking out loud again. "Hmm, fired. At camp. Fired. Camp."

"OMG," Stacia says, with a huge emphasis on the G.

"What?" Turner is looking at Stacia, as most of us would look at the village idiot when he starts yelling about enormous floating blue elephants attacking city hall.

"Campfire. The campfire is laid out in a circular pattern, remember?"

She's right. I remember thinking the 12 huge tree stumps looked like the face of a clock. "Eureka! You nailed it. The leader stump is larger than the others too. That's our 12:00."

We race for the door and I hear Carrie say "Eureka" under her breath. I'm not altogether sure if she's mocking me or trying the word on for size. Either way, the word fits.

When we step into the night, the rain has stopped, the hail has disappeared and outside of the frequent lightning strikes, it is a beautiful evening. The lightning flashes make the courtyard resemble the set of a movie. And I don't mean a feel-good romantic comedy type of movie. I mean a scare you so much you're peeking through your fingers, too scared to look, too scared not to look type of movie. You know the genre, where the crazed stalker with the hockey mask is terrorizing a group of college students. Yeah, it feels a lot like that. But on the plus side, the rain has stopped.

Getting to the campfire site at Glenn Park means crossing the swing bridge again and traversing that bridge at night is not good. Not quite halfway across and I've long since kissed my comfort zone goodbye. These bridges are not safe. When have you seen one of these in a movie and something hasn't gone horribly wrong? The rope snaps, the plank breaks and suddenly someone is plummeting to their untimely death. I don't want to be that person.

Yet, I'm the first to start across. I gave directions for Stacia to follow when I am two-thirds across. It's no accident I chose Stacia to follow— she is the lightest member of our group. No way am I sharing the swinging rope bridge of death with Turner, who must weigh at least 50 pounds more than me.

My main issue becomes apparent quickly: it's difficult to keep moving when you have a death grip on the rope railing and your fingers have absolutely zero inclination to loosen up. It's clear my fingers have an unusually strong instinct for self-preservation. The only way I made it across was through the power of positive thinking and telling myself, You can do this. You CAN do this.

Oddly enough, the others appeared to have little-to-no difficulty navigating the narrow deathtrap. Maybe they aren't as tuned into the other side. Go figure.

Finally, reaching the campfire site at Glenn Park, we are without the light from our usual comforting fire, and long shadows obscure the area as the night has reclaimed the grounds. Not wanting to prolong our time here at camp spooky, we quickly head for the stumps. Orienting myself, I point out, "There's the leader stump. That's 12."

We move counterclockwise. "11."

"10, not 10 the clue said."

"Here. 9:00. This is where it should be." We gather around the stump, running hands along the rough sides feeling for our clue in the darkness.

I sense it before I hear it. I can feel a presence nearby. We are not alone out here.

If there's one thing you probably have learned about me by now, odd things are attracted to me. The once-in-a-lifetime happening, well, that's a Monday for me. The bizarre appearance of some unknown entity, welcome to my Tuesday. Wednesday will bring something equally strange—and you don't even want to know about the rest of my week. I have no idea why I am such a magnet to this type of thing, but to dispute the obvious will get me nowhere.

I know we face an imminent threat, as clearly as most would know there is a seed stuck in their teeth. What's unclear is the nature of the threat. I need to know who or what we're facing. Standing up, I scan the surrounding darkness.

Figures move slowly in the shadows, circling us, always moving, like a wolf pack stalking prey. I can't make out who—or what—they are. Strangely a number pops into my head. Five.

There are five of them out here. I remember catching a glimpse of five figures earlier outside of the University Center. The fact we were put into groups of four must have jarred something in my head, my brain taking note of the oddity. Why would there be five? What I don't know, is if the five are from our world—or from the next. What I do know is there are only four of us.

I don't think the others have picked up on the danger yet. "Guys," I say quietly. "We are not alone out here."

There is a shuffle of gravel off to my left. "Death awaits you all with sharp, pointy teeth." The voice quiet, barely above a whisper.

Behind me, Stacia makes a noise. It sounds like a whimper. I don't turn around.

"What is it?" Turner asks, his voice trembling.

"I'm not sure," I say as the figures steadily circle us.

"What do you want?" Carrie calls out.

"Death." The whisper is off to my right this time.

"Sharp." My left now.

"Pointy," the whisper's behind me.

"Teeth." Directly in front of me now.

I consider myself a student of pop culture. I read People, surf the entertainment blogs, watch a lot of cable TV and catch some classic movies. A favorite of mine is the classic Monty Python and the Holy Grail. Towards the end of the film, there's this great scene where the brave knights face a killer bunny. The knights quickly realize they are over-matched and amid shouts of "run away," they do exactly that. I remember the lesson well, knowing there will be times—when faced with insurmountable odds—that the best course of action may well be a strategic retreat. I have to say, at this moment, my fight or flight instinct is strongly tipping in one direction.

A random thought pops into my head. In the same film, a strange little man had warned Sir Robin and his brave knights of the killer bunny. "Death with nasty, large pointed teeth."

Now hold on for a moment. It's not a ghost I'm hearing, but I do smell something fishy here. "Tommy?" I call out.

"There is no Tommy, only death," the voice hisses.

"You are such an idiot," Stacia says with a laugh. "Tommy, I would know your arrogant voice anywhere. Nice try."

A solitary figure separates from the shadows. It is Tommy—the jerk. Stacia and I get a solemn nod while he gives Carrie an appraising look and totally ignores Turner. There is no love lost between those two.

"Got it," Turner says, scroll in hand. "Let's move."

Stacia stands in front of Tommy, hand on hip, bouncing side to side, giving what I assume is her best flirting move. "Sorry, hun, we gotta go. We have a contest to win." She pushes past him.

"Hey, Tommy," I say as I follow Stacia. The other four boys step out from the shadows. Standing behind Tommy, they look less than friendly.

Carrie and Turner are behind me. They eye Carrie up and down while she returns their gaze with an aloof appraisal. With a dismissive eye roll, it's obvious they do not meet her standards. As Turner attempts to follow her, the boys close ranks around him. "He stays," Tommy says, putting a hand on Turner's chest.

He is not the same charming soccer boy we met in the cafeteria. Gone is his ready smile, and gone is his flirtatious manner. What remains is a lot darker than I have seen before. As Tommy glares at Turner, the muscles in his jaw clench, his tension mounting. There is a rising storm of malice in him threatening to erupt at any moment. For his part, Turner holds his ground, neither provoking nor turning away from the threat facing him.

I realize there is more going on here, more than just super-charged testosterone coming to a head between these two. I sense an outside influence; something is unquestionably interfering here. The question is where the outside influence is coming from. Over the years, I've come to believe another dimension coexists alongside ours. This dimension is inhabited with the deceased who have not yet found their way or who have returned for some purpose that only they know about. This dimension is not just a transitory place for dead people—there are other things existing there. I have caught the occasional glimpse of dark fleeting shapes, terrifying figures watching from the shadows. These glimpses are the stuff of nightmares.

Don't get me wrong, there is more to this dimension. Wherever there is shadow, there has to be light. I have glimpsed other beings that fill me with near indescribable warmth, leaving me with a peace so serene nothing short of a tornado plucking me from the ground and sucking me into the darkness would break my new found calm.

Most of the time, this dimension parallels ours, not intruding into our dimension. But not all the time. Some of the inhabitants are stronger than others, and these are constantly seeking weaknesses, searching for a way into our world. When a vulnerability is discovered, they exploit it, often finding a vibration tuning them into our world. And this allows them to influence and interfere with the living.

Have you ever met anyone who likes to cut themselves? I have. This otherwise normal girl was using a razor blade to cut her arm, opening her skin repeatedly after the wound began to heal. When I asked her why, she wasn't able to give me an explanation. This self-mutilation made no sense until I saw something looking back at me from her eyes. There was a dark fury staring back at me, challenging me. What I saw in her eyes was not from our world—at least not from the world most people live in.

Sadly, this is exactly what I am seeing in Tommy. Something is exerting control over him. Exactly what the new Tommy is capable of is the question running through my head. How ugly can this get? A violent reaction from him is certainly on the table. Protecting Turner has to be my priority—he has no idea what is actually happening here.

"Tommy, hun," I say, stepping up to his side. I run my hand down along his arm, feeling the cords of his muscle tensing up. I'm ignored for the moment as he continues his staredown with Turner. I need to break his concentration, disrupt his focus before this gets ugly. Giving Tommy's bicep a hard squeeze, I continue. "You have such large muscles—for a soccer player."

My obvious sarcasm has the desired effect as Tommy's head slowly turns in my direction. I push on Tommy's right arm with my left and just as he turns his body in my direction, I bring my knee up as hard as I can. I've seen this done in the movies and was hoping it would have the same effect. It does. Based on the sound he makes as he collapses, and watching him rolling on the ground with both hands shoved between his legs leads me to believe that he may be in some discomfort.

I point a finger at the closest of Tommy's buddies. Holding his gaze for a long moment, I growl, "You don't want to mess with me. Not this week."

He looks a little shaken and holds up his hands. The others take a step back, no longer looking me in the eyes. There is no fight left in these guys. That's okay, I'm done with them anyway. Turner steps over the stricken Tommy as we make our exit.

26 | DON'T YOU JUST LOVE DARK BASEMENTS IN DESERTED BUILDINGS?

We are still laughing a block later. "You were amazing," Stacia says.

Even Carrie seemed impressed. "I had no idea you were so tough," she says. "He won't be getting up anytime soon."

"Unbelievable," Turner says. "What was up with that guy? I've never liked him, but he was acting so bizarre."

"Could be the bad weather bringing out the worst in him," I offer. "I had an uncle who used to cry every time it snowed."

"Really?"

"Yeah. He was depressed half of the year. The other half of the year he was so worried about the upcoming winter, I don't think he was ever really happy. He finally listened to the rest of the family and moved to Florida."

"Did that help?"

"I don't know. He was run over by a bus the first day he was there."

Stacia looks at me, a scowl on her face. "And this entire time I believed you were the odd one in your family."

A thought stops me. "Did we get the clue? I might have to kick their butts again if I have to go back there."

"I have it," Turner says, holding up the scroll with a smile, the ribbon is not blue like all the others. He slides the red ribbon off. "I guess this is our final clue of the hunt," he says.

We crowd around to read the verse as Turner unrolls the scroll.

> *You shouldn't throw stones if you're mad,*
> *And happy people won't climb this tree,*
> *Don't worry about the final answer you seek,*
> *You will find it low in the NW corner.*

Huh?

"That is so obvious," Carrie says.

I am missing something then. "It is?" I ask her.

"Well, duh. If happy people won't climb a tree, who will? Crabby people, that's who. Crab tree. Crabtree Hall. There you go," she says rather smugly.

"Isn't that building off limits? I'm pretty sure it's posted as closed for construction." Stacia says.

"You know, I thought I remember seeing a sign to that effect," I offer, thinking of our earlier visit there. "Would they send us into a building closed for construction?"

"It does seem unlikely," Turner says.

I decide to approach this logically. "What about the throwing stones part? What does that have to do with Crabtree Hall?"

"That is just a throwaway line to get us from the mad people to the happy people part. You're reading way too much into this," Carrie says, arms folded, as she steps into my space, staring me down. Carrie can be one intimidating bitch when she wants to be. Fine. Whatever. "Crabtree Hall it is then," I shrug.

What kind of a person throws stones? The question runs through my head as we break into a run for Crabtree Hall. No answer comes to mind as we turn the corner and see the building silhouetted by a flash of lightning. Not exactly looking like it came out of a travel brochure, the lighting makes the campus building look rather ominous. The windows are all black, the only trace of light a faint glow coming from the front entrance. My breath catches in my throat as I see a familiar slime-green glow coming from an upper-level window. The symbol is back. The glow is faint at first, but it quickly becomes bright, as if someone has turned the dial way up. I glance at the others to gauge their reaction, but they don't appear to notice. Turning back to Crabtree Hall, I am shocked to see the symbol now glowing brightly from every single window in the entire building. The symbols are burning so brilliantly that I find myself squinting as I try to take in the mystery before me. The others—completely oblivious—move down the sidewalk to the entrance. I admit it: I'm more than a little freaked out. The brilliant glow rapidly dims and fades from sight altogether as I approach the entrance. Okay, message received. If only I knew what it meant. A random thought pops into my tired brain. I know who shouldn't be throwing stones: people who live in glass houses.

Carrie slips off her backpack and drops it by the front steps. "We shouldn't need this," she says, pushing past the building's closed for construction sign and lifting up the yellow caution tape at the entrance.

If I didn't know better, I would think they were trying to tell us something. But closed or not, we are going inside. The faint light I saw earlier in the entrance is a construction light hanging over a wooden table littered with blueprints and coffee cups. We pause just inside the lobby area.

"Which way do we go?" Stacia says.

"The northwest corner."

"Which way is that?" Shrugs all around.

Turner steps up to the table and peers at the blueprints. He twists the plan around, sliding his finger around the paper getting his bearings. "Okay," he says looking up, "that way is north, and west is that way," pointing down a dark hallway. Not exactly inviting.

Turner flips up the blueprint, revealing another set underneath. "Hang on, there is a lower level. The clue said low in the northwest corner. It looks like the basement is where we are supposed to go."

Great. I love dark basements in deserted buildings. Good things always happen there, right? I have faced down a lot of terrifying things in the course of my short life. That doesn't mean I have to look forward to seeing more. However, I remember a quote I once read in my English class. You become brave by doing brave things. I turn on my way-too-small flashlight, leading the way into the darkness. Time to be brave.

The hallway is an obstacle course of ladders, tools, various pieces of construction equipment, and even segments of walls. Most of the floor and some of the walls have been stripped down to bare studs. This part of the building is getting much more than a facelift. I lead the group down the hallway carefully, watching every step. The symbol showing up so prominently on the outside of the building hints that there is something here, something I need to be cautious of. The symbol is so mysterious—and besides giving me the willies—it doesn't tell me anything. Like any good girl scout, I do my best to be prepared for whatever drops my way. That's all I can do.

The stairwell is as gloomy as a graveyard and my flashlight barely makes a difference. The beam illuminates a tight circle at my feet, but when I aim it down the stairs ahead of me, it's as if the darkness swallows the light. The only way to navigate the stairs is to shine the light onto the step below and follow the light. With each step down, the air feels colder around me. My internal spookometer edges up another notch or two. The others are behind me, quiet outside of their breathing. No one has said a word since we moved into the darkness leaving me to wonder if they are sensing the same ill-at-ease feeling I am.

A metal door looms in front of me. The door leads into the basement level, and hopefully, our final clue will be there waiting for us.

Do you ever have a song just pop into your head? Usually, when it happens to me, it's some annoying song sticking around for hours before it finally leaves—no doubt off to bother someone else. This time, it's a classic rock song, "You May Be Right," by Billy Joel. My mother would often play his Glass Houses recording when she was cleaning up the kitchen. She said it gave her energy to do her chores. Even though it has been several years now, I remember the CD cover. It had Billy Joel looking all tough in his black leather jacket, getting ready to heave a rock through someone's window. Mom said Billy Joel was trying to be edgier, but I think he was attempting to distance himself from his soft rock ballads. Either way, the recording had some decent tunes on it. Hmmm. Glass houses.

Hand on the doorknob; it hits me: we are in the wrong building. All the clues point in that direction. You don't throw rocks if you live in a glass house, and the university is well known for their research on crabapples. I'd forgotten about it, but there is a glass house on campus—a greenhouse used for crabapple research. I would bet my iPhone the greenhouse is where we should be, not this smelly old dungeon of a basement. But there's no reason not to check here first, is there?

I pull the door open with a supreme effort, as it creaks loudly, protesting every inch of the way. I would guess this door hasn't been used for decades. The funny thing is, before coming to this camp and enduring the seemingly endless physical training sessions, I wouldn't have had the strength to muscle this door open. I'm not saying I could punch out the Hulk, but I have muscles where I didn't before. I straighten my arm, checking out my bulging triceps in the light of my flashlight. Very nice.

"Um, Abbey?"

"Sorry." I push through the doorway and stop. Though I feel someone bumping my backside, there is no way I am going further. There are three figures ahead in the darkness. The lead one is an older woman. Her face lined and stern, hair severely pulled up into an old-fashioned bun, this woman could make a living as a librarian. The woman's clothes looking even more out of style than her hair, but it's difficult to be certain when you can see right through them. Her torso is mostly transparent—less in our world than in the next—but her head looks to be more solid. It is an eerie sight. The two figures flanking her are large men with folded arms standing behind the old woman. These men belong to the shadows; it's not so much a matter of transparency, they simply do not belong here in a world where there is light.

The woman raises her hand and stabs the air with her finger. The gesture is clear: *go back*.

"Abbey?" The voice is Stacia's.

I look around, my flashlight illuminating Stacia's, Turner's and Carrie's faces. There is little doubt they see something too. The emotions slide over their faces like the "How am I feeling?" poster in Ms. Neuman's office. Shock, fear and wonder pass through in equal amounts. I reach out my hand, touching Stacia's arm. "What do you see?"

Stacia looks at me with an odd expression as she hesitates, and gestures past me, "There's a woman's head. I can't make out anything else; her body just fades away—except for her hand."

Turner speaks now. "I think there are others with her. I'm certain really—it's just that I can't actually see them."

"She wants us to leave," Carrie says. "Maybe we should." Her voice trembles as she says this.

Stacia looks at me. "Is this what you see, Abbey? There is an old woman here, right? I mean you see this type of thing fairly often..."

I can feel Carrie and Turner's eyes on me. Not wanting to meet theirs, I keep my gaze on Stacia. "Yes, I see the woman. And two others are standing behind her. I can't make out much beyond their shapes, but I believe they're men. I get the feeling they're here to bring power to the woman. But they don't want to be seen—they don't belong in our world."

Stacia's eyes are watery as she holds mine for a long moment. "Have you seen the woman—or the men for that matter—before?" I shake my head. "What do you want to do?" she asks.

"I think we should leave. Now," I say firmly.

"But what about our clue?" It's Turner this time.

"It's not here. It's at the school's greenhouse."

Carrie's mouth hangs open, but it's Stacia who asks the question. "Why didn't you say something if you knew?"

I hold up my hands. "The thought just occurred to me as we got down here. I..."

That's the moment all hell breaks loose—and enters our world.

Simultaneously with an echoing boom, the building shakes with a frightful groan. Living in Minnesota, I've never experienced an earthquake. Tornadoes, yes. Complete whiteout snowstorms, even with thunder, yes. I've been affected by floods, chased by a cloud of mosquitoes, been threatened by an angry bear and even been given the evil eye by a protective mother moose as I maneuvered my canoe past her and her calf in the boundary waters of northern Minnesota—but I've never been through an earthquake. Sure, I've seen them in the movies—with the violent camera shake, the protracted shudder of the ground heaving and the side-to-side pitching of the people involved. This is not like that. At all.

The boom is all around us. I can feel it through the floor, up my legs, all the way to my teeth. The shake of the building is sudden and violent, almost as if we're being hit by something. But what?

Though no one is beside me, I hear a whisper right next to my ear. It's oddly intimate to have someone this close. I half expect to feel the warm breath in my ear, it's that close. The whisper is not a sweet caress to my senses, though. It's more of a life-saving message, a warning of an immediate threat. There was only one word used. But it's enough. "Run."

"Go," I yell, propelling Stacia back through the doorway. "We have to go!" I grab onto Turner's shirt and put a hand on Carrie's shoulder, pushing them ahead of me. "Move!"

The explosion is massive. It's loud and it's catastrophic. I feel the shock wave as the concussion blows right by the doorway. The deadly debris propelled by the blast's concussion narrowly misses us as I'm sent sprawling to the floor. In the process, the flashlight falls out of my hand and hits the wall, causing the light to wink out. Luckily, I no longer need it to navigate. We now have a new light source: the explosion started a sizeable fire just around the corner from us. It's close and burning tremendously hot. The heat of the flame quickly sears the paint on the doorframe.

"We have to get out of here. This building isn't going to be standing much longer." My voice is ragged and loud as I shout to be heard over the roaring fire. The stairwell is filling with smoke, a thick, black cloud looking twice as toxic as an over-microwaved Hot Pocket. Or worse. With only one way out, we hurry up the stairs. It won't be long before the smoke takes us.

Instinctively, we grab hold of each other's hands, a human chain to get us through the gathering darkness. Turner is in the lead, pulling me by the hand, Stacia is behind me holding my other hand in a near-death grip with Carrie brings up the rear. My mind flashes back to younger days, holding hands with the girls, singing, "Ring around the rosey, A pocketful of posies. Ashes, ashes. We all fall down." Katie, Jean and I rolling on the ground, giggling uncontrollably. Hannah Scout always first to her feet, shouting to do it again, do it again. Friends I haven't thought of for years, friends I haven't seen in forever. Friends I hope to see again—in this life.

I'm trusting Turner with my life as he leads us up the stairwell. The positive thing here is that with nowhere else to go, there's no place to get lost. We simply have to move up the stairs to get to safety. Looking back over my shoulder, I see great billows of black smoke pumping into the stairwell. With each passing second, my vision is getting more and more obscured. It's becoming harder to breathe with all of the smoke and I am choking as I try to get some air into my oxygen-starved lungs. Turner bends down, getting a breath of fresher air and I follow his lead, squeezing Stacia's hand so she gets the idea too. For the next few moments, we are this weaving, dipping chain, attempting to survive this horrible situation.

My foot is confused as it reaches up for the next step and finds none. However disconcerting this may be for my foot, it's good news for me. We are finally at the landing, and it's just a quick run down the hallway to freedom. The stairwell has filled up with so much smoke I doubt we'd have made it up to another floor. Turner yanks open the door and we're almost out of here. Or not. That's the trouble with life—it's never as simple as we might imagine it.

There is a wall of flame ahead of us.

27 | HIGH STRANGENESS

I knew I should have bought that life insurance. It's beginning to look as if my stay at camp may be shorter than I originally had thought. No matter how badly I wanted to leave, getting carted out in an ambulance or a hearse is not the way I want to go. When I go, I want to go my way.

At the moment, our options are looking severely limited. There is absolutely no way we can go back into the stairwell and we can't go through the wall of flames either. The flames look to have come up through the floor from the basement. The explosion's resulting fire has grown immensely, leaving me wondering how much longer this building will stand. So, what do we do?

Carrie pushes open a door into one of the dorm rooms. "The window," she yells. "We can get out through the window." There is a roar coming from the hallway as the fire consumes everything in its path—a path we appear to be in. Me? I'd like to choose the path less traveled. The window it is then.

Unfortunately, the window is one of those that doesn't open—just a large double-thick piece of glass. I guess they don't want the college students sneaking out at night. Our situation becomes even direr, as smoke floods the room—the fire right outside the door. Turner slams his shoulder into the window trying to break the glass. Nothing happens. He takes several steps back, before running at the window. The glass bows a bit, but the only real result is Turner being flung to the ground. He looks dazed as he gets back onto his feet. The flames are licking at the edge of the doorframe, not quite into our room, as they curl around the edge. Clearly, we don't have much time left.

Close to panicking, I frantically look around the room for something to break the glass. This is a construction site, there has to be something we can use to bust the window open. But the question is, will busting out the window send a load of oxygen into to a hungry fire? The answer is clear, we have no time and we have no choice.

I spot a bucket at the base of the scaffolding set up along the far wall, handles sticking up out of the bucket. I race over, hoping to find a hammer. Hand on the orange scaffolding, I glance up to see an opening right through the ceiling.

"Hey," I call. "Over here."

Stacia is first over. "Forget the window, we can climb right out of here." And just like that, she's moving like an Olympic athlete up the scaffolding. It's amazing what you can do when you're properly motivated. Carrie and Turner start up after her. Stacia has no trouble whatsoever making it through the opening. Turner has to work at wriggling through, and I have the impression Stacia is pulling from overhead. Maybe I could push him from this end …

The moment is gone as he makes it through, quickly followed by Carrie. I am struck by the similarity to our obstacle course as I make my way up. A last glance down shows me the fire has entered the room. Time to make my escape.

Hands are waiting for me as I reach through the opening and I am pulled up to the second floor. In a decidedly awkward moment, we all embrace in a group hug. It feels so good as tears run down my cheeks. After an uncomfortably long moment, we let go and back away from each other. This room is pretty much the same as the one below with a noticeable difference: there is no fire. We may have bought ourselves some time, but not a lot.

We make our way into the hallway, relieved not to find the fire here—yet. I still smell smoke, but it's probably just me. You know how you smell all smoky when you get home from a bonfire? It's like that—only a thousand times worse. The others look both wet and sooty, and I imagine I look just as lovely. But hey, this is a scavenger hunt, not a beauty contest. However, at least for us, the hunt is over, it's just a very real game of survivor now. And this is not a game you want to lose.

"We need to get back down to the main floor," Turner says. "It's our only way out. Let's go to the far stairwell and make our way down. It should be far enough from the fire. Are you with me?" he asks, looking at each of us.

I nod my head along with Carrie and Stacia. What other option do we have?

Running down the hallway, I'm thinking there's no way my father is sending me back to camp next summer. Not if I have any say in the matter. And now that I have my own lawyer, Brian Thompson, attorney at law, I have double the say. Look out, Dad.

We're running down the hall just passing the elevator bank when I see it again. I hit the brakes and yell, "Hold it!" at the top of my lungs. When Turner hears me, he reluctantly stops and reverses direction. He sees I've stopped and have no inclination to continue.

"What is it?" he asks, looking a little wary of the spooky girl. I feel that's my role here once again. Being that girl has cost me more friends than I can count on both of my hands—and yours. However, I can't ignore a warning when I see one. Turner steps closer, a questioning look on his face. I simply nod at the door adjacent to the elevator.

The mysterious symbol—a sickly shade of green—is glowing brightly on the door. The curved backward letter f shape, with the dot at the bottom right, looking as if it was hacked into the door with an axe—not delicate and definitely not subtle. "Look at the way it's glowing," I say. "It has to mean something, doesn't it?"

Carrie reaches out a tentative hand toward the mysterious mark. As her finger makes contact with the door, something decidedly odd happens. The glow jumps from the symbol and attaches itself to her fingertip. Carrie utters a frightened moan but leaves her hand where it is. Time grinds to a halt, my breath caught in my lungs as I take in the high strangeness unfolding in front of me. The glow expands engulfing Carrie's entire finger, then gaining speed as it takes over her hand up to the wrist. She turns with terrified eyes, pleading with me to make it stop. But there's nothing I can do as it rapidly moves up her arm. Her t-shirt sleeve flutters and bulges out as the glow has seemingly taken on mass. It's moving higher up her outstretched arm, almost to her shoulder now. Carrie's sudden, piercing scream galvanizes us and sends time back to its normal pace.

As one, we all move to help Carrie. Stacia has her hand around Carrie's waist pulling her back, I'm slapping her hand away from the door and the strangely consuming symbol. At the same moment, Turner is making a full body tackle to get her away from the door. The result is we're all thrown to the floor, a tangle of bodies, which rolls us into the opposite wall with a bone-jarring thud.

Before we can get to our feet, a massive shudder rocks the building and the end of the hallway we were headed for collapses. No explosion, the ceiling simply buckles and falls into the hallway, causing the floor to give way. Flames engulf much of the falling debris, as though another fire had been raging on the top floor as well. The noise reminds me of a locomotive bearing down the track at full speed. When the roar is over, the entire end of the building is a jagged tear, exposing the building to the night.

I can't even begin to describe the sight of the lightning flashes as they light up the hallway. The rain is pelting the hall's interior, sizzling as the drops strike the smoldering debris of what was just recently the third floor. "Oh my God," Carrie says, "Abbey, if you hadn't stopped us ..." Her words trail off.

Turner is getting to his feet. "We'd all be dead," he says finishing Carrie's thought.

Maybe it's not so bad being the spooky girl, after all.

28 | LOUD WOMPF SOUNDS ARE NEVER A GOOD THING

What do you do when everything is crumbling down around you?

No, I'm not speaking figuratively or even metaphorically here. I mean the entire frickin' building is on fire and falling down around me. Literally.

"We've got to get out of here." Carrie says this matter of factly—as if we haven't all been thinking the same thing. "This firetrap won't be standing much longer."

"Yeah, but how?" Turner asks, a look of near-panic coloring his face. "Every way we go is another dead end."

I hold his eyes for a long moment, willing him to feel my calm. I glance to the others. "You're going to have to trust me. I believe I can get us out."

"But how?" Carrie this time.

"I think we've been getting some help and I've got to trust we won't be led down the wrong path." My fingers are crossed for good luck, but I'm not going to share my superstition with the others. "We start with this door," I say, hand on the knob.

"Are you nuts?" Turner asks. "No offense, but why are you trusting whoever is sending these messages? Why would someone—or something—want to help us? I think you're too trusting for our own good."

"Suppose they want you to cross over to be with them? That seems more likely," Carrie says and pauses, a decidedly awkward pause. "Just saying..."

I feel the tears wanting to flow, but now is not the time. "Let me ask you this," I say, looking directly at Carrie. "What choice do we have?"

Blank looks of indecision all around. That's what I thought. "Follow me, if you want to live." I've always wanted to say that. I push open the door and step into the darkness.

So what are our options? We're on the second floor, with one floor above, a massive fire spreading alarmingly fast in the basement level below. The building is laid out with stairwells on opposite ends and one in the middle, located next to the elevator. We're at the middle stairwell and the only path to our escape is on the first floor, so we automatically turn to the descending stairs. Large metal drums fill the landing below, making it difficult to pass through.

I glance up, seeing the now familiar symbol emblazed on the wall above the flight of stairs. "We can't go down," I say, grabbing Stacia's hand and pulling her toward the greenish glow of the symbol. Wouldn't it be easier if they just put up some arrows instead? Same idea, right?

Life is strange. The symbol's glow has given a bizarre greenish-lime cast to the entire stairwell—making us look like some type of Jello creatures. Strange times, indeed.

The mark begins to fade as we approach the landing halfway up to the third floor. When my foot hits the landing, the symbol has disappeared, leaving us in the dark. Confident we're being led up to the third floor, I shuffle to my left, outstretched hand sliding along the wall as I turn toward the rising stairs. Yes! The glow is burning brightly at the top of the stairs. It may be the strangest beacon ever, but it's my beacon. "C'mon, Stacia, we're almost there."

Without warning, there is a loud wompf sound below us. I don't know about your life experiences, but in mine, loud wompf sounds are never a good thing.

Turner heads back down the stairs. "Hang on," is all he says. We lose sight of him as he turns the corner. We look at each other, not sure what to do. How long is he planning on being gone? We don't exactly have much time here.

It turns out he is thinking the same thing. Eyes blazing, Turner comes around the corner, frantically gesturing at us. "Run!" he shouts. The panic in his voice takes away any indecision we might be feeling. "Run," he shouts again. We don't need to be told twice, we're running for our lives.

Fire inspectors will later confirm the wompf sound was an enormous fireball caused by the ignition of chemicals stored on the second floor landing. I'm no building inspector, but storing 50-gallon drums of chemicals in a stairwell would be an obvious safety code violation in my book.

We bust through the symbol-marked door onto the third floor, anxiously scanning for another otherworldly mark. For me, this has become so much more than just escaping; I want to know what these symbols mean. My mom used to talk about her harrowing experiences in South America. Being in such a strange land had frightened her at first, but, "Curiosity will conquer fear even more than bravery will." I get that now. The symbol had shown up before our lives were in danger. It has to mean something beyond being our roadmap to safety, and I will not stop until I figure it out.

"There," I shout. The symbol glows on the wall not even ten yards away. As we race in that direction, the mark fades as a new one lights up the wall another ten yards down on the opposite side. There is smoke in the hallway, but with the building opened to the night air, there is more than enough ventilation. Of course, the necessary components for fire—heat, fuel and oxygen—are now present in copious quantities. Ahead of us, the last third of the building is alive with dancing flames. Yet, this is the direction we're heading in.

The symbol fades as if someone is rapidly turning down the dimmer switch. Another ten yards down, the symbol glows brilliantly—from a door this time. With no hesitation, we hit the door, ramming it open. The room has been stripped down to bare studs, the flooring removed to the support beams. Stopping at the edge, I can see down into the second floor room below.

Stacia is frantically unlooping great lengths of an orange industrial-weight power cord, as Turner grabs one end and races over to the bare studs of the closest wall, looping it around the beam. Tying it off with three knots, Turner pulls tight using his weight and bracing his shoe against the beam. Satisfied, he rejoins us as Stacia tosses the remaining length over the edge. "Go," he says, directing me to go first.

I grab the cord and fall through the opening. My hands, now used to climbing ropes, easily hang on as I quickly slide down to the second floor, landing gracefully. Stacia follows, letting out a whooping cheer as she flies down the cord. Leave it to Stacia to make the most of each moment. Carrie rockets down and Turner practically jumps the whole way, using the cord to put on the brakes at the very last second, cushioning his landing.

Safely on the second floor, we continue our quest to find a way out of the building. Stepping out into the hallway, I size up our options. The floor has been completely removed directly in front of us. Ten feet down the hall the floor looks passable, but there is no way to leap that gap. Turning back to the others, looking for ideas, I notice the green symbol glowing on the wall behind Carrie. That's it.

"We have to go through the wall. The hall is blocked." The time for disagreement is long past. The others simply nod and begin to look for the appropriate tools to get us through the wall. The sledgehammer seems just right and I grab the handle, surprised by the weight.

"Allow me," Turner says, and I relinquish my grip on the handle. To say Turner attacked the wall would be an understatement. Zero hesitation, he launches himself at the wall, swinging the sledgehammer wildly. The fear and frustration fuel his intensity to Hulk-like savagery. The drywall doesn't stand a chance. He's through the wall with the first swing, the second swing creating an opening large enough for us to squeeze through.

Turner's fury doesn't readily release him from its ferocious grip. He's pulling back for another hit. I step in and grab his forearm, stopping him at the apex of his swing. "You've got it," I say gently. "Let's go." He throws the massive tool to the ground; like yeah, I'm done with you.

The adjacent room is much the same as this one. Stripped down, an opening to the room below—an opening to a room on the first floor. This could be our way out.

The door, however, has the symbol. I have to trust it. We have no choice but to go right after we go through the door. The gaping hole in the floor is to my left, as well as the collapsed end of the building. The smoke is thick out here, almost as thick as it was in the stairwell. I turn back to the room, taking in a large gulp of air before stepping back out.

Ahead, just over an arm's length away, another symbol is on the wall. With visibility so limited, I'm thankful the mark is close enough tor me to see it. There's something about the quality of the glow that cuts through the smoke, much like fog lights illuminating the way through the mist. Another symbol on the opposite wall, and another opposite that. We weave through the smoky corridor bouncing from wall to wall. After about the seventh wall symbol, I see it on another door.

This door is locked, but there's no way we're letting that stop us. When you're as highly motivated as we are, a locked door is nothing. Turner steps back, bracing himself against the opposite door. Everyone should know how to bust open a door by now. We've all seen the cop shows. Turner's technique is spot on, as he lunges forward and slams his heel into the door next to the knob. The door flies open, the latch plate gliding across the room, bouncing off the wall. So cool.

Looking over the edge of the opening in the floor, I see the welcoming glow of the otherworldly mark down below—far below. What's not so good is the fact the mark is not on the floor below, but on the one below that. We're being led back to the basement.

"Turner," I say looking into his sooty face, the streaks looking much like a warrior's face paint before battle. The similarity is not lost on me, as we have been battling for lives for the last hour. Honestly, it may have only been ten minutes—time seems irrelevant in circumstances like ours. "We have to go back down to the basement."

No argument. He simply nods, holding up a flashlight. "I found this with the tools."

"That helps. Now we just need another cord. A really, really long cord."

Carrie comes up with the power cord—yellow this time—and hands the end to Turner. Seconds later, I'm freefalling into the abyss wondering where and how I may land. I recognize this as a metaphor for my life, just as another of my mom's sayings picks this moment to pop into my brain: "To expect the unexpected shows a thoroughly modern intellect." Believe me, with my life, I always expect the unexpected.

On the way down, I slide, tightening my grip to slow my plummet, and slide again. It's an odd experience to rappel through a room and continue through the floor into the room below. I can only imagine the surprised looks I would get if someone was sitting in the first floor room, perhaps a man sitting in his overstuffed chair reading the paper, watching as I go shooting through his room. However, there's no one—alive at least—in this building. I'm gaining speed as I head for the basement level.

I hit the concrete floor of the basement with a bone-jarring jolt. The smoke is thick, though the fire isn't right on top of me. I step to the side as Stacia drops through the ceiling hole, making that whooping sound again. Honestly, if we weren't in such danger, this might be a little fun.

With Carrie and Turner's arrival, I spin around looking for the symbol marking our way out. I hold no illusions that with the building falling apart all around us and the fire consuming what's left, there's no clear path out. We need to find that symbol to get out of here. And we need to get out soon. As if to punctuate our pressing need, the floor shudders, a loud creak that turns into a groan and quickly crescendos into a full-blown roar. The ceiling collapses directly behind me. I spin around, totally stunned at what I see. It's massive, the entire end of the building where we first came down the stairwell, is starting to resemble a landfill littered with the remains of construction materials. A compressor falls right in front of us, no doubt having been on one of the higher floors. It positively explodes on impact, launching a thousand pieces in our direction. One of the wheels hits me just above my knee.

"Move," Turner yells grabbing my arm, propelling me down the hall. "This whole building is coming down and we're underneath it all." A sprint for the finish, we're racing away from certain death, with no idea where we're headed. No symbol has shown itself as of yet.

We're roughly in the middle of the building, near the elevator and adjoining stairwell moving fast. There are more flames and a wall of debris ahead.

I almost miss it.

Down low, back in the dark, I see a faint glow, a familiar greenish glow. The symbol itself is not visible, but that scary, awful—yet wonderfully welcome—lime green glow is there. "Here," I call, as I hit my brakes. "It's down here."

Turner's flashlight lights the way, past a sea of crates, and years' worth of stuff, because nobody knew what else to do with it—other than shove it into the basement—is a little tunnel. Set back maybe three or four feet at floor level—is a square metal door. The door is roughly three square feet in size. Cobwebs surround and completely frame the small door, showing us it has been years—more likely decades—since anyone has used this long forgotten door.

Yet, the symbol is glowing through the cobwebs from this very door. The mark itself looks to have been made by someone who had a screwdriver and plenty of time. I can see the scratches and grooves, dug deep into the metal of the door. If I had done this, it would have taken well over an hour of painstaking time, scratching over and over, digging the pointy end of my screwdriver into the steel of the door. After that, I would've taken a can of green glow-in-the-dark paint and coated the etched symbol until it radiated brilliantly from the center of the image and a more diffused glow from the outer edges. In case I haven't made it obvious, someone clearly not from our earthly world has placed this symbol here.

29 | A SPOOKY GIRL LIKE ME

It's going to be gross and disgusting, but I know exactly what I have to do.

"Let me go first," I offer. No argument from the others on this one. Down on my knees, I use the handle of Turner's flashlight to clear away the cobwebs until I am inches away from the door. "Here," I say as I hand back his flashlight. I won't be needing it anymore.

"Eww, gross Abbey," he says when he touches the mat of sticky webs on his flashlight.

Reaching out with my right hand, my fingers inch tentatively toward the etched glow of the symbol. As it did with Carrie earlier, when I make contact, the glow jumps from the symbol and onto my fingers. With my frightened nerves screaming at me to pull away, I force my fingers against the symbol as the sickly lime green color spreads up my fingers, overtaking my entire hand and quickly enveloping my arm. I feel a cold tingling sensation as the glow spreads, almost as if the warmth is being sucked out of my skin.

"Abbey," I hear Stacia gasp behind me.

I can't stop now, realizing this is the only way. Inching forward, I press my palm flat against the symbol. The cold spreads faster, moving up my neck now. I can't help but shiver as the glow completely covers the upper half of my body.

Even though my arm feels like it's getting the early stages of frostbite, there is raw power in my touch. I squeeze my fist, enjoying the sensation. Reaching out and grabbing onto the door's rusty handle, the glow from my hand seeps into the handle and trusting my otherworldly helper, I twist and pull in one confident motion.

With a feeble, creaking protest, the door opens. The second my hand had touched the door, I knew—without a shadow of a doubt—that I could open it. There appears to be more going on here than I first suspected, as strange thoughts begin to flood my head—faces, someone running, emotions and different languages. Everything is going so fast, too fast to comprehend as the film races by in my head. A whirlwind that only seems to speed up. Images of foreign looking faces, exotic locales, screams, pain. Hot. Cold. Darkness.

Willing it to stop, I focus my breathing, using the meditation techniques my mother taught me. It takes everything I have, but I am able to push it all away. The rush of intruding thoughts and memories slow and go dim. Shivering now, I stretch my arm out into the tunnel, the supernatural glow illuminating a surprising distance ahead. There is no end in sight, just shadows becoming darkness. We have no real choice, though. This tunnel is where we have to go.

I'm maybe ten feet into the tunnel from the entrance, trying to avoid skinning my knees, but it's a losing battle. Wearing shorts seemed like a good idea at the time. There just isn't room to move in here—other than the slow forward crawl I'm already doing. Stacia, followed by Carrie and Turner, are behind me. Someone behind me is crying, but seeing as I can't turn back, I have no idea who it is.

"I still think we can win this thing," I call out in an attempt to lighten the mood. "Really, the scavenger hunt is ours. I'm guessing none of the other teams have had the help we've had. And so what if we lose? Could extra physical training faze us after what we've been through? No frickin' way!"

Turner calls back from the rear, "Mr. Johnson better not even try. I have some pranks I've been saving that will blow him out of the water. He won't know what hit him."

That a boy. Keep their minds off our current situation. If we panic in here, it could potentially be as dangerous as if we had stayed in the building. We have to stay focused on what lies ahead. Never mind the collapsing firetrap we've left behind or this dark, damp, and utterly claustrophobic tunnel we're trapped in. We just have to think about getting out.

"A root beer would be good. What better way to celebrate than with a tall frosty mug?" Stacia says. "A root beer, and maybe some french fries. Sounds perfect, doesn't it?"

Carrie chimes in, her voice lacking its usual confidence. "I am thirsty. Breathing in that much smoke leaves a girl quite parched."

"I could go for an ice cream cone," I reply. "Our favorite place is Nelson's Ice Cream in Stillwater. There's nothing else like it and nothing quite compares. There are holes in the ground, and there is the Grand Canyon. There are songwriters, and there are Lennon and McCartney. There's food in this world some people call ice cream, and there is Nelson's. The size of their cones is astonishing. A child's size cone would feed a family of four. And Stacia...they have root beer too."

"I'm in."

"Me too. So let's get out of here."

"Sounds good," Turner calls. "Can you go any faster?"

"I'm trying," I reply. My bloody knees are moving as fast as they can.

And in his best Yoda voice, Turner answers, "Do or do not, there is no try."

The tunnel feels as if it stretches on forever. I have absolutely no idea where we are, how far we've moved away from Crabtree Hall—or even if we've moved off campus. We could be across the Kinnickinnic River by now. Who can tell when you're deep underground? I'm tired, my knees are raw, my arms are sore, but the supernatural glow radiating from my hand has not diminished in the least. It continues to light the way. I'm hoping I will see something different soon besides the never-ending shadows ahead, some sign that our underground journey is coming to an end.

And then, here it is.

The tunnel has come to an end. The shadows ahead close in as I make out another steel door, a twin to the one miles behind me. I grip the handle tightly and twist. Again it opens easily, this time out into a chamber. Crawling through the doorway, I am relieved to find myself in a tall space. There are metal rungs attached to the sheer concrete wall. Extending my arm to light the way, I see a dozen of these metal steps and another door at the top. This is it!

Stacia's head pops out of the doorway. "What's going on, spooky girl?" No malice, no teasing, just her friendly banter.

I grin at her. "Looks like we made it."

"I know, right?" She holds out her hand for some help, and then seeing my glowing hand reaching toward hers, pulls back. Not that I blame her. "I got it," she says and pushes her way out.

Carrie takes Stacia's offered hand and slides out of the tunnel. Her knees look as bad as mine. "Nice work, spooky," Carrie says, her face breaking into a grin.

I suppose I may have just taken on a new nickname. Understandable, considering I'm glowing like nuclear-radiated lime Jell-O. "Thanks, Carrie. We're a good team, aren't we?"

"The best." Her eyes look wet like maybe she's tearing up. You know, I could actually grow to like this girl.

"Hey, don't forget about me," Turner says as he pokes his head out.

Stacia tousles his hair playfully and smiles. "Never, big guy. You da man. We couldn't have made it without you. Now, come on out so we can go collect our trophy."

Turner squeezes his wide shoulders through the narrow doorway and, standing, stretches to his full height. "I thought we would never get out of there. I will never watch another prison break movie where the prisoners tunnel out," he says, shaking his head.

I have to laugh. "Have you seen many prison movies?"

He shrugs. "Well, no. Just making a point, really." His voice trails off.

"You are a goof, but I love you," I reply before realizing what I'm saying. The others are quiet, shifting glances between Turner and myself. Talk about your awkward silences.

Turner is the one who breaks it finally. "I love you too, Spooky." Which works, as everyone cracks up laughing. I'm laughing too, but underneath this glowing green light, I'm pretty sure I'm all red with embarrassment.

30 | SWEET RELIEF

At the top, I hesitate. I'm confident my hand's on the door leading to our freedom. What I am not so confident about, is how my supernatural glow will go over when others see me. Let me spell it out for you: for a 14-year-old girl, life is all about fitting in, not calling attention to yourself. Yeah, I get what you're thinking, not being like everyone else should be a good thing. My dad likes to say, "To wish you were someone else is to waste the person you are." However, it's one thing having your own sense of style, it's another thing altogether to be glowing like Dr. Frankenstein's Jell-O dessert, made after a long and hard night in the lab.

Stacia, who appears to be able to read me like a book, accurately understands my hesitation. "Abbey, it's going to be okay. What we've survived tonight… it's amazing. Don't let a little thing like a little extra color ruin things for you."

"Extra color? Extra color would be a sunburn, not this mutant glow. I look like one of those fish from National Geographic that lives in the dark at the bottom of the ocean."

"Let's just get out of here," Stacia says, sounding confident and reassuring. "We'll get it sorted out. Somehow."

Not quite so confident, I grab the handle above and push the door open. Immediately, I am slapped in the face by an angry shrub. The opening is overgrown with bushes—Willie, the groundskeeper, clearly hasn't been doing his job—and I have to fight to create enough of an opening for me to get through. The night air smells so clean and fresh—no small wonder considering we were trapped in a burning building and forced to crawl through a moldy tunnel. Climbing out, something remarkable happens. My glow simply fades and disappears. Yes! I pump an arm into the air, though deep down I'm so relieved I could just cry. It's tough keeping it all together some days. And this would be one of those days.

We step out of the bushes and try to get our bearings. Sirens fill the night air. It must be every fire truck in the entire county. They are close and more are coming. One goes screaming by, just over the rise of trees.

"Let's go," Turner calls out over the wail of the sirens. Re-energized, we race for the top of the hill. And stop.

"Unbelievable."

"Whoa."

"We were in there?"

We are standing in a line, side by side, at the summit. Stunned at what lays before us, we instinctively reach out for each other's hand. I'm not even sure whose hands I'm holding, but it doesn't matter. Drawing on each other's strength, we try to process what we are seeing.

Crabtree Hall is engulfed with flames, reaching a hundred feet into the air. Both ends of the building have completely collapsed. The middle section remains standing, but the top floor has collapsed onto the second floor. This is where the fire is burning the hottest, whereas the ends look to have mostly burned out. Smoke is pouring out of the rubble. Fire trucks surround the building, as the firefighters work urgently to contain the fire. Police cars and medical vehicles are on the scene as well. A crowd of curious is watching from across the street.

Still stunned at the sight of the devastation before us, we slowly approach the crowd from the back taking in the commotion playing out across the street. The firefighter's efforts are focused on the middle section, and another two trucks arrive and join the fray. It's a spectacular sight to see the truck's ladder extended to the second story and a stream of water hitting the fire.

I try to shift position to get a better view of the action. There's murmur building quickly from the group and people are pointing as a firefighter runs up the sidewalk to the entrance. He scoops something up into his arms and races away from the building as a portion of the second floor collapses, raining debris onto the front steps. I join the collective gasp of the crowd, stunned to see just how close to death the firefighter was.

He joins the men directing the firefight at a red SUV parked askew on the curb. After a moment of collaboration, the firefighter is pointed across the street. He pauses long enough to remove his helmet and wipe the sweat from his forehead, concern evident on his face. Almost reluctantly, the firefighter crosses the street heading toward the crowd, still carrying something in his left hand.

Mr. Kindle, Mr. Johnson and Ms. Neuman, as well as several of the camp staff are standing in front near the curb. Some of the ToughLove campers squeeze in behind trying to hear what's being said. Standing here in the back, I can't hear anything, but I can see the firefighter's face as he talks to the staff. Whatever he was carrying is handed over to

Mr. Johnson. Ms. Neuman moves closer, looking to see what it was. Her normally impassive face contorts with emotion.

A murmur ripples through the group. I want to know what's happening, so I whisper to the girl in front of me, "What's going on?"

Without turning around, she replies, "They found a backpack. Guess one of the scavenger teams was inside when lightning struck."

Ahh. So that's what happened. Lightning. That certainly explains the enormous boom. Looks like my fear of storms has been validated, for once. Oddly, I get no comfort from the thought. It took me way too long to overcome the paralyzing fear of bad weather. That fear is no longer welcome in my life. Besides, lightning never strikes twice, right? The odds have to be astronomical that I would endure another killer storm in my lifetime. From now on, I can live a charmed and stress-free life. Sweet.

Turner is beside me. I feel for his hand, and his strong fingers intertwine with mine. "What's happening?"

"They found a backpack. A scavenger hunt team was inside when the lightning struck. It was lightning that started the fire."

"That makes sense."

"Who was inside?" Stacia asks, joining us.

"Not sure. They found someone's backpack."

"Hey, that's my backpack," Carrie says, "I left it on the front steps."

OMG. "Everyone believes it's us in that building—they think we died in there."

Turner leans in. "This is too cool. Let's go, let them think that for a while. And then we can just show up. Imagine what the reaction will be." He tugs on my hand, pulling me from the scene. I let go of his hand, knowing I can't leave.

I'm watching Ms. Neuman, her face holding my attention. She's crying. The entire time I've known her, I wondered if she liked me at all. At times, she seemed so aloof and distant, while other times I thought she was mean. One thing I'm confident about—seeing her sobbing in the midst of her peers—she is devastated at the news of our deaths.

I push my way through the group, knowing I have to go to her. Ignoring the stunned faces of the people I pass, I move to the front of the group. Her head down, Ms. Neuman's body quakes with the emotion of her sobs. I reach out, touching her cheek, wiping away her tears. "I'm okay," is all I can think to say.

She lifts her head, her eyes looking into mine, shock and surprise giving way to sweet relief. She grabs me and holds me close like she will never let go. I can feel her sobbing. It's a moment I will never forget.

31 | I'M THE SPOOKY GIRL

"Un-frickin-believable!" I'm shaking my head.

"One week left. One more week here at our favorite Camp ToughLove." Stacia is lying on her bed, looking straight up at the ceiling. "Our lives will never be the same."

I have to agree. The aftermath of our near-death experience has been overwhelming. When we were discovered, you'd think we threw the buzzer-beating, game-winning basket from half court. People were yelling, crying, lifting us up, and hugging us until I thought my insides were going to come out my ears. The crowd surrounded us as we told our story, each of us relaying portions of the journey through the burning building. Thankfully, none of us made mention of the ghostly symbols road mapping our way out. That would have been nearly impossible to explain. The head firefighter looked a tad skeptical hearing we just happened to find the needle-in-a-haystack way out. "How would you even know it was there, let alone know it would take you out of the building?" Lucky guess.

Mr. Kindle confirmed I was correct about the clue being written to point us to the greenhouse. And surprisingly, he agreed the clue was vague enough to point us at Crabtree Hall as well. The shocker came when he addressed the crowd, citing our teamwork as the model of how we should be working together for the common good. "Harriet Beecher Stowe once said, when you get in a tight place and everything goes against you till it seems as though you could not hold on a minute longer, never give up then, for that is just the time and the place the tide will turn. These four embody that spirit better than any example I could dream of." Imagine, me, a positive role model.

The staff wanted us to go to the hospital, but we were having none of that. "I feel fine," each of had insisted in our own words. Really, none of us wanted to be separated. We had been through too much together to go our separate ways. Even Carrie stood with her arm around me for support as the firefighters and camp administrators grilled us about the night's events. And to tell the truth, I was okay with her being so close. When you risk your life together, a bond is created that is unbreakable. Carrie will be my friend for life.

"Hey, guys," Carrie and Turner pick this moment to stop by our room. The last thing said as we finally parted last night, was we would meet up for breakfast. For once we hadn't woken up at the crack of dawn as our physical training regimen has been put on hold, possibly for the remainder of camp. Surprisingly, I'm torn on this, because as much as I have disliked physical training, I wouldn't have survived last night without it. Cows will fall and you have to be prepared for it.

"Carrie!" I yell and crush her with the passion of my hug. A week earlier, I would have bet a million dollars against our ever hugging, let alone voluntarily being in the same room. It's the near-death bonding thing again. "Abbey!" she yells, matching my forceful hug with the same maximum pounds-per-square-inch death grip. I have tears again, but it's okay, these are my friends.

"I'm here too," Turner says, looming next to us. Carrie and I open up and make a Turner sandwich, squeezing him between us.

"Hey, I want some too," Stacia says as she joins us. It feels nice, really nice.

After breakfast, we're back in our room, still talking about last night. It's a lot to process. Turner clears his throat, hesitates and asks, "What about that symbol? We haven't talked about it, but..."

The others look to me. Stacia, always the direct one, asks, "This is your area, spooky girl, what does it mean?"

I shrug. "I honestly don't understand it. Whoever—or whatever—wants to convey a message." For a while now.

Turner reads my unspoken thought. "But you've seen this symbol for a while, right? It hasn't been just in the Crabtree firetrap." He looks at me, his eyes conveying his warmth.

I nod.

Stacia perks up. "I saw it before, too. It was like someone had drawn the symbol with a finger on Abbey's sheet. And it was on the wall of Charlotte's classroom. You said you both watched it being drawn onto the wall."

"Yeah, that was the first I'd seen of it."

"Peas," Turner adds, "it was on your plate of peas."

"Peas?" Carrie asks. "Really?"

I'm smiling now. "My father always told me not to play with my food. So I'm at dinner the other week, and I look down to see that a ghost has been playing with my food. It would have been funny if the circumstances hadn't been so scary."

"It was a little funny," Turner says with a grin. "If someone's trying to get your attention, that certainly worked."

"It's not as if the others were hard to miss," I blurt.

"Others?"

Looking down, I suddenly find my toes to be especially fascinating.

"Others?"

"Well, there have been a few. On the bathroom mirrors, backstage at the theater and on the windows—every window actually—of Crabtree Hall."

"Really? Why didn't we see those?"

"I would guess they weren't meant for you." I'm the spooky girl, remember?

Carrie is on her feet, pacing the small space. "Let me work this out. We each saw the symbol during our escape from Crabtree Hall. We were meant to see them because we needed to see the symbols to escape. Someone wanted us to survive what most certainly would be a deathtrap. That makes sense, but Abbey, you started seeing the symbol before our rescue. Someone wants you..." Her words trail off. The room is silent as Carrie continues her pacing. "Someone wants you to..."

Carrie stops her pacing, and kneeling in front of me, takes my hand. Looking into my eyes, she offers, "Abbey, whatever the symbol represents, it means something for you. And only you. This feels personal, not like some random spirit from the other side is here messing with you. I love you, spooky girl, and I know you'll figure this out. Somewhere, possibly deep in your memories, the symbol is there. And when it comes to you, everything will make sense."

I just hope it happens soon.

32 | LATE NIGHT DOODLING

It's 2 a.m. and I can't sleep.

My mind races without respite, as the recent events play out repeatedly in my head. The startlingly vivid images, sounds and emotions from the symbol's glowing transference revisit me. As before, it is too much to process. Holding my breath for a long moment, I begin to control my body, slowing my breathing, slowing my mind, gaining control. Meditating on these strange thoughts, I'm now able to examine them.

Faces, someone running, emotions, different languages. I can't understand what is being said, can't recognize the language, but I know the joy that's expressed suddenly turns into fear. Shouts—that feel more like commands—echo in my mind. The images of foreign looking faces and exotic locales are familiar, even though I'm certain it's nowhere I have visited.

Focusing my breathing, I'm able to slow it down even further, replaying it like a film from the beginning. This time, I'm consciously examining every frame searching for the symbol. Because these strange thoughts sprung from touching the symbol, it would make sense the symbol— and the meaning behind it—would be revealed to me. However, sense doesn't appear to have a part in this—the symbol is not here.

Frustrated, I sit up. The clock glows 3:13. Clearly, sleep isn't an option tonight. Ms. Neuman said when you can't sleep and your mind is racing, you need to remove things, not add them. She said writing out your thoughts is the best way to remove things, while reading and watching TV usually makes things worse as they add things.

Flipping on my reading light, I open a notebook to a blank page. My pen sits on the first line, poised for action. However, the words don't cooperate. Unsure how to start, I begin to doodle subconsciously. My pen slowly draws an elegant looping line down and across the page. Lifting the pen, I bring it three quarters of the way back up and let the point rest on the paper. Almost by itself, the pen moves horizontally across my original line leaving behind a shorter wavy one. Lifting the pen, I bring it to rest just to the right of my vertical line. The pen sits there, waiting. Waiting.

It's at this moment I become aware of what my doodle has become.

I shouldn't be at all surprised. What else have I been dwelling on forever? And I don't feel as if I've made any progress whatsoever. Out of anger, I throw the notebook across the room, watching it hit the wall and slide to the floor—the symbol face up, mocking me. Ughh, I just want to scream. It looks like Ms. Neuman was wrong this time, this has not helped me go to sleep. Just the opposite.

All hope of sleep abandoned, I grab the CIA's Guidebook to Venezuela and sit on the floor leaning against my bed. Starting from the back, I flip through the pages, not really reading the words. My mind is moving too fast to read. The images of Venezuela pop out at me as I speed through the book, page-by-page, chapter-by-chapter. Moving this fast, I'm more absorbing the pictures than studying them.

The feeling comes roughly three quarters of the way through: I've been here before—which is crazy, because I haven't. In all the travels with my father, we've never been down to South America. I suspected he purposely avoided taking assignments bringing us anywhere that could remind him of my mother's disappearance. Not that she was ever very far from my thoughts—or likely his as well. The question remains: why does it feel so familiar?

I continue my rapid pace through the book, flipping through each page like a high school boy's first Playboy magazine. This blistering pace continues until I reach the executive summary at the front of the book. The section is laid out by geographic region, featuring a satellite image with an overlaid map detailing each area, along with highlights of that specific region.

My finger has paused, resting on a map. I recognize the region as the ultra-violent area near the Colombia border—the area with the mass amphibian kill that so freaked out Stacia and me earlier. Another coincidence? My finger traces along a river, as I think about all those dead frogs killed by the drug making chemicals dumped into the river. 50-gallon drums of poison poured out up here, killing everything along the way, as the chemicals make their way down to here. The drugs are bad enough, with most destined for the US, via Colombia's cartels, but to ruin the environment for years to come with no regard for the native Venezuelan people ....well, that's just wrong.

As my finger traces along the river's path, I stop. And scream.

33 | THE RETURN OF BRIAN A. THOMPSON, ATTORNEY AT LAW

Stacia is out of bed, frantically scanning our room for the threat. Her wide eyes looking for the source of the screams. There's no knife-wielding homicidal maniac. No ghostly figure with hands wrapped around my throat, squeezing the life from my body. Just Abbey, the spooky girl from Woodbury, Minnesota.

"Oh my God, Stacia. I know."

"Know what, Abbey? What is it?" Her confusion apparent, her concern obvious.

"I need to talk to my dad. Right now." I'm lunging for the bedside table, looking for my cell phone. Speed dial #2 gets my father's phone ringing. As before, it frustratingly goes to voicemail. "Dad, I need you right now. Please call the second you get this. It's a matter of life or…well, a matter of life." A recorded voice comes on, telling me my father's voicemail is full and my message wasn't retained. Son of a …. I slam the phone down.

Now what? Who can I tell? No adult is ever going to believe me. My eyes hold Stacia's, her concern turning into worry. "Abbey…"

"Who's going to help me, Stacia?"

"I'm here…" she offers in a tentative voice. No doubt believing her roommate has gone far, far off the deep end.

"I'm here… to help," I echo. Yes! Frantically scrolling through my call list, I find his number and hit the call button.

"Abbey, it's 4:30 in the morning. Who are you calling?"

"Brian A. Thompson, attorney at law, of course. He can help. He has to."

The voice on the other end is thick with sleep, but still recognizable. "Brian Thompson, attorney at law. I'm here to help."

Thank God.

Not many adults would even listen—let alone believe—a frantic 14-year-old girl at 4:30 in the morning. Yet, at 7 a.m. sharp, Brian A. Thompson, attorney at law, is at my door. "Hello, Miss Hill," he begins. I grab his collar and pull him into our room. Patience is not my strong suit this morning.

Rapidly telling the story, I hold nothing back. Other than an occasional raised eyebrow, my attorney, Brian A. Thompson, appears to believe me—which is strange, as I barely believe it myself. However, deep down I know it's true. Every word. There's absolutely no other explanation.

My attorney is very professional, taking notes—on a legal pad I presume—and asking clarifying questions as he draws more information out of me. Stacia is quiet the entire time, nodding her affirmation as the Crabtree Hall events unfold. When his questions appear to be entirely answered, Brian A. Thompson sets down the pad and leans forward. "Before I was an attorney, I had another life. I was in naval intelligence for twenty years. When you spend that much time working in intelligence, you get to know a lot of people in similar capacities within our government. In those circles, as well as in adult life, favors are traded to help each other meet their objectives. Lucky for you, Miss Hill, I made way more deposits into the favor bank than withdrawals."

On his feet, Mr. Thompson says, "No promises, but I'll make some calls. It's an hour later in Washington, so I should be able to reach someone—though these types of people don't tend to sleep much. I'll be in touch," he says, shaking my hand and walks out with my book under his arm.

34 | SAYING OUR GOODBYES

The morning sun shines through my window, introducing me to my last day of Camp ToughLove. Adrenaline propels me from my bed, no lingering for this girl. This is going to be a big day.

"Wake up, Stacia," I say giving her a shake. "Today's the day. Last day here."

The adrenaline hits her too and she rolls right out of bed, landing awkwardly on the floor looking much like a hot dog rolled into a crescent roll. We're both laughing as she struggles out of her blanket prison. "Hey, it's not easy being me you know," she says with playful exasperation. "You try it for a day."

"No thanks, there's already too many of you." She shoots me one of her looks. I know when I get that look, I've scored a point with her. Stacia is all about the witty repartee. My banter has definitely improved after spending the summer together. To tell the truth, I'm confident my life will never be the same.

The funny thing is, I always thought my life was okay. My dad and I learned to cope—and thrive actually—after my mom's disappearance. Life changed, we adapted, and I became good at some things, got really good at avoiding other things and life just kept living. Smooth and steady. But let in some friends, allow yourself to share fears and feelings and you begin to grow. And then there's the physical aspect. You never know what you're capable of until you push yourself, competing with others—and yourself. I've gained tremendous strength and confidence from the challenges I've faced. I wouldn't recommend anyone risk their life the way I have, but it does have profound aftereffects. Your perspective changes, it has to. When you see what's important—the really important things in your life—you have to think differently. The quest to fit in, popularity, what to wear or not wear, the near constant worry about what others will think about you...well, it just isn't that important anymore.

The end of camp comes with not so much a bang—been there, done that—but a whimper. Mr. Kindle and the rest of the camp leadership are addressing us outside the University Center. We're fidgeting on the hard metal folding chairs facing the front steps as Mr. Kindle speaks.

"Camp ToughLove is about love. Most of you have had difficult lives, faced difficult choices and unfortunately had difficult results. Because someone loved you—or maybe it was a court appointed representative—a choice was made that brought you here. That choice brought you to us.

"Camp ToughLove is about personal responsibility. We are the ones responsible for each choice we make. It's not other people or events that are responsible for the way we think and feel. It is your life, and you are in charge of it.

"Camp ToughLove is about strength. As our Ms. Neuman likes to say, there will always be falling cows. Life isn't always going to be smooth and predictable. She tells the story of a family driving underneath a cliff and a 600 pound cow dropped onto their new car. A foot or so over and they would have been dead. In your life, kids, cows will drop. You won't see them coming, and you won't know what happened until it's over. The only thing you can do is accept it and roll with whatever life throws your way. Hopefully, we've made you physically and mentally strong enough to deal with life's difficult circumstances. It's how you react to adversity that makes you who you are. Becoming a whiner, saying that life isn't fair—or worse, running to your overprotective parents—will get you nowhere. Remember, it's your life. Take charge and deal with it."

Mr. Kindle pauses, looking around the group, attempting to make eye contact with each of us. This goes on for a very long half minute. "Camp ToughLove is about working with each other. Many of you are here because of your inability to relate to others. Let me tell you, being an angry loner is not all it's cracked up to be. You need other people. It's that simple. God put you here on this planet to be with other people. And I don't mean simply co-existing with each other—our relationships matter. I've learned that people will forget what you said, people will forget what you did, but people will never forget how you made them feel. Be a blessing to others and your life will be immeasurably richer."

I look over my shoulder. There are a number of parents and families listening and waiting. Scanning the new arrivals, I search for my father. He is nowhere in sight.

"We want to thank you for giving us your summer." Turning back, I see the staff fanned out across the landing, all holding hands. "We realize it may not have been your choice to be here, however this could be the summer that changes your life forever. All we ask is that you allow yourself to be changed. Ms. Neuman will offer our closing prayer."

Changing places with Mr. Kindle, Ms. Neuman leans into the microphone. "Please close your eyes and bow your heads." After a brief pause, she continues, "Heavenly Father, we want to thank you for each and every soul that is here. Be with each of your children as they go back out into the world. Wrap them up in your loving arms and help them to realize they are not alone in this world. Help them to find others to lean on, as well as others who need their new found strength. We ask that each child of God here will go out and become a light for you, taking whatever life throws at them and let them shine magnificently just as coal becomes diamonds under the highest heat and the heaviest imaginable pressure. Bless each child, giving them purpose, filling them with your strength, your hope and your love, allowing them to become the change our world so desperately needs. In your son's name, Amen."

Mr. Kindle's next words are the most welcome words of my summer: "You are dismissed. See you next year." A cheer rings out through the University Plaza and welcome chaos reigns. Families swarm, hugs and tears flow. Making my way through the crowd, I still can't locate my habitually late father. When he dropped me off, he said he would be here, promising his assignment would be completed in time. I hope he was correct.

"Abbey," I hear my name. It's Carrie with a big hug and a bigger smile. "These are my parents and this is my big sister, Jenna." A pleasant looking family stands behind Carrie, offering warm smiles.

"Nice to meet you all," I say. "I wouldn't be here now if it wasn't for

Carrie pushing me the entire summer." Wrapping her up, I give her a big squeeze.

"That's Carrie," says her sister, Jenna. "She's always going to push you."

"I love this girl," I say. "She can push me anytime."

"You have my number, so stay in touch," Carrie says. And she is gone. I will miss her.

Stacia finds me with a squeal and lunging tackle-like hug. "I am not saying goodbye," she says with a tear. Her emotions thicken her voice. "I will see you this weekend. You are, and forever will be, my new sister."

"Truly," I say with a wink.

"Oh no," the blonde woman behind her says. "You didn't bring out your fake French sister, did you? Oh, Stacia. What am I going to do with you?"

I'm laughing as Stacia scoops up her little sister. The dark haired girl gives a joyous shriek. "I love Truly! She's funny." This makes us all laugh and it feels very, very nice.

I'm walking through the thinning crowd, still a fatherless orphan. He will be here. Of that I have no doubt. There is someone else I'm searching for as I make my way through the happily reunited crowds. From the look on Turner's face, he has been searching for me as well.

"Abbey," he says with a nervous formality, "I would like you to meet my father, William Dalton." A stern faced man with a military-style haircut steps forward thrusting a calloused hand into mine.

"It is a pleasure to meet you, Miss Hill. My son has been telling me about the challenges your group faced together. By all accounts, it was a harrowing experience. Turner said you played a significant part in the successful outcome. Thank you."

"Sir, I can honestly say without your son's ingenuity and support, I would not be standing here today. I've never seen anyone who can improvise and think on their feet as quickly as your son. You should be proud of the man he has become." I hold his gaze, using the strength of my will to get him to acknowledge Turner's contribution. It seems to work.

Mr. Dalton steps next to his son, putting an arm around Turner. It takes a long moment, but he looks at Turner, "I know I don't say this enough, but I am proud of you, son."

"Thanks, Father," Turner says. "Could I get a minute with Abbey… to say goodbye?"

"I'll give you two," Mr. Dalton says without a trace of a smile.

Turner takes my hand and pulls me to a bench. Still holding my hand, he looks into my eyes. "Abbey, I'm not sure what to say. I just don't want it to be goodbye."

"Turner, maybe we should stay friends. You are someone I can talk to, someone I trust with my feelings. And I haven't had anyone like that for years." It's tearing me up inside to say this.

Turner's shaking his head. His eyes hold mine. "Love is friendship set on fire, Abbey. It's everything that friendship offers and more. You won't lose our closeness or your safety net. Love takes all that we have and makes it deeper, fuller, and more alive. I used to sleep a lot, but not anymore. For once in my life, my reality is better than my dreams. You have to be the most amazing girl I've ever met and I don't want to lose you."

Wow. He is really good at this. I am sweating, and yet I have goosebumps. It sounds like the flu, but more likely, it's my turbocharged hormones. I touch a trembling hand to Turner's cheek. "Let's stay in touch and see what happens. I do love you, Turner Dalton."

I don't know how it came to happen, Turner leans in and...it's amazing. His soft and tender lips are on mine and I am transported to a warm, wonderful place. A place where I could get totally lost. That is until...

"Abbey?" It's my father.

35 | WHAT KIND OF CHURCH CAMP IS THIS?

"Daddy?" Trying to re-engage my brain, I look up to see a most welcome sight. "Daddy!" I scream and wrap him up in a bear hug, which he returns with equal passion. I'm crying as all the emotions of the last two months flood out like a broken fire hydrant.

"Sweetheart, I missed you too. I wished I could call, however, the arrangement mandated no calls out. My cell was confiscated on day one and I still haven't gotten it back. Funny story," my dad says with a smile, "apparently the duty sergeant who took it had the worst case of diarrhea..."

"Wait, Dad. Didn't you hear my messages? You have no idea what happened?"

My father looks perplexed. "Umm, no. Anything important?"

I look over at Turner, who's turning tomato red trying to hold his laughter. His coughing fit is enough to set me off and I burst out laughing. I'm wiping away tears, trying to regain my composure. However, one glance at my father's confused face starts me laughing again. I'm drawing a crowd now, as Kirsten, Corey, Amanda, Brooke, Ms. Neuman and Charlotte surround us. For once, it doesn't bother me to be the center of attention. I'm relieved to see Stacia and Carrie squeeze their way through to join us.

Leave it to Stacia. Stepping up to my father and throwing her arms around him, Stacia shrieks, "Daddy!" The look on his face is priceless, as his outstretched arms don't seem to know what to do. Eventually, one hand gently pats her on the back. Too funny.

Carrie slides an arm around me, "Hey there."

"That's my dad," I proudly tell her.

Nodding, Carrie says with a grin, "I guessed that."

"Dad, these are my friends, Carrie and Turner. I see you've already met Stacia," I say smiling.

Extricating himself from a very clingy Stacia, my father, smiling uncomfortably, says, "Stacia and I go way back."

"Yeah, maybe two minutes," Stacia says as she finishes his joke.

Looking as perplexed as having three Qs and trying to figure his next word in one of our Scrabble games, my father asks, "So what went on here? It must have been exciting."

Turner steps up. "I've got this one. We were assigned into groups for a scavenger hunt and our group—me, Stacia, Carrie and Abbey—ended up in a deserted building by mistake. The building was struck by lightning, starting the entire building on fire leaving us trapped in the basement. The fire inspector later told us the lightning hit the top floor, but the current surged through the cabling and blew out the electrical system in the basement causing an explosion and fire. Your daughter was able to lead us through the maze of fires, blocked hallways, and collapsed floors. And she found the needle-in-a-haystack tunnel out of the building, just as the whole thing was collapsing on top of us. Simply amazing."

I give my father a knowing smile. "I may have had a little help, if you know what I mean," I say with a wink.

Putting a weary hand to his forehead, he replies, "Oh, man. Yeah, I believe I know what you mean." He looks at Turner, Stacia and Carrie, who give him solemn nods in return. The rest of the crowd doesn't have a clue what actually happened in that building—and I want it to stay that way.

Quickly looking to change the subject, I happily add, "But everything ended well, right? We may not have won first place in the hunt, but we were given a special camp award for teamwork and overcoming adversity. And at a handy 8-1/2 by 11 size, I've been told it's suitable for framing."

Carrie jumps in, too. "All that military-style physical training actually paid off. I don't think we could have made it through the fiery deathtrap without it."

My father has regained his perplexed expression. "Military-style physical training? What kind of church camp is this?"

This time, I'm not the only one laughing. It's pretty much the entire group, as most know the story of my father's mistaken camp registration. "Umm, Dad," I start. That is until a honking Jeep speeds around the curve and comes to a rather abrupt stop at the curb. I recognize the driver. It's my attorney, Brian A. Thompson.

36 | THE SHORT CHAPTER

"Hey, Miss Hill," Mr. Thompson shouts as he leans through the open window. "Miss Hill!" He is furiously waving and for good measure hits the horn again to catch my attention. It works, he has my full attention.

"Who is that?" my father asks.

"It's my attorney," I say as I jog down to the Jeep, completely unprepared for the shocking sight.

My wind is completely knocked out and both knees pick that moment to buckle. Mr. Thompson's quick reactions are the only thing that saves me from a less than graceful face plant into the door of his Jeep. My mind is racing, yet I have no possible idea what to say at a moment like this. Fortunately, my mom does. "Hi, Abbey."

37 | SOMETIMES IT'S REALLY GOOD

Sitting on the other side of my attorney, is my mother.

Looking at me with her incredibly bright eyes is a very much alive Dr. Katherine Hill. Ever since I told Mr. Thompson the symbol's meaning, I've hoped and prayed she was alive. After seeing the ghostly symbol repeatedly, and finding it matched up perfectly to the river in western Venezuela, I knew she would be alive. And the sense of urgency I felt wouldn't have been there otherwise.

I want to go to her, but I stand rooted in place and Mr. Thompson is talking to me. "You were right, Abbey," he says. "The spot on the map next to the river was the rebel guerrilla camp where your mother was being held captive. They were using her as their own private physician. A special ops team was able to spot her right away and with the help of a clever diversion, she was rescued and airlifted out. Believe it or not, the hardest part was getting someone to believe a small-town Wisconsin attorney having credible intelligence about Colombian guerrillas operating inside Venezuelan borders. But like I said earlier, some important people owed me a favor."

"Abbey?" It's my father approaching.

"Daddy, I found Mom. She was..."

"Constantine!" My mother is running around the end of the Jeep toward my father.

"Katherine?" The complete range of possible emotions surge across my father's face and settle in on relief, pure sweet relief. And he grabs my mother and simply holds on, holding her like he never would let go of her again. It is absolutely beautiful.

I give them their moment and then join in. My daddy is crying, my mom is sobbing and I completely lose it. Looking into my mom's face, there are new lines, the last several years obviously have been hard ones. But it is the most welcome face in this entire world. "Thank you so much, Abbey," she says touching my cheek. "Brian told me everything on the way over here. I know you hate what you have, believing it a curse. I'm here to tell you, it's not. You have a gift, Abbey. A wonderful gift."

Wiping away my tears, I nod. "I know, Mom. It's part of me. It saved our lives here this summer." I gesture to my friends. "Without it, none of us would be here."

My mom gazes at me, a tender look in her eyes. "So you had some help?"

"I'm convinced it was Grandma leading me out of the burning building. It took me awhile to figure it out, but she showed me where you were, too. She had been trying to send me a message for a while. It had to be Grandma."

"That could be, she always looked out for us. I'm also pretty confident she's passed her gift onto you."

My attorney, Brian A. Thompson, steps up to us. I surprise him with a hug, my feet off the ground. "Thank you so much. I don't know what I would have done without you. You are the best attorney in the entire world. I don't think I could ever repay you."

"Well, there is the matter of my bill," he says with an envelope now in his hand, an unreadable expression on his face.

"We've got that," Ms. Neuman says, stepping forward. "It's the least we could do for you, Abbey."

"Thank you, but it's not necessary," I tell her. "If there was one thing worth paying for, it's Mr. Thompson's legal fees."

"It's only a dollar?" Ms. Neuman says, with the opened envelope in hand, confusion on her face.

"Only a dollar," my attorney, Brian A. Thompson says with a grin. "Miss Hill qualified for my student discount. I have payment plans available, as well. Though, I think your credit is good." I love this guy.

"You know, I have a strange idea," I say to the group. An idea, like a ghost, must be spoken to a little before it will explain itself. "Despite almost dying in the middle of our scavenger hunt, despite the grueling physical training, the possessed soccer players and even the field of squishy dead frogs, I will miss this place." As I look around at my new friends, I finally begin to understand why. Maybe my idea isn't so strange after all.

My father is looking around, a goofy smile on his face—the weight of the world now completely lifted from his shoulders. "This certainly is an odd church camp, isn't it?"

Laughing, I put an arm around him and my mom, squeezing them tight. "You have no idea."

Sometimes it's really good to be the spooky girl.

ABOUT THE AUTHOR

Allan Evans has written professionally in advertising and marketing for over a decade. He currently is a writer for a publishing company.

A soccer coach, he can usually be found on a soccer field somewhere, teaching kids about soccer and life.

Allan lives in White Bear Lake, Minnesota.

Follow Allan on Twitter at EvansWriter.

Email Allan at allan@EvansWriter.com.

Visit Evanswriter.com.

Abbey is back in **Scary Clowns,** the sequel to **Spooky Girl.**

Ever since I was a little girl, I could see things that others couldn't. These things are spooks, ghosts, dead people, call them what you will. They seem to be attracted to me for some reason; I'm sort of a spook magnet. It's not as glamorous as it sounds—I hate dead people.

But it gets worse. Something bad followed me home from the circus. I've been seeing clowns all around our school—and not the funny, big shoes, red nose sort of clown. No, these are scary clowns. And now in the midst of a clown apocalypse, lives are in real danger. And it's up to me to stop them.

Available at Amazon.com.

Made in the USA
Lexington, KY
24 May 2018